Boy

Also from EATMS Productions

Books on power, survival, women's autonomy, and the systems shaping modern America.

Nonfiction

Billionaires, Capitalism, and Power

Evil and the Mountain Ungreed
Self Help for American Billionaires
Selfish Steve and the Ivory Tower
Tariffs, Taxes, & Face-Eating Leopards
Ban Billionaires: Fascism Fix

Fascism, Religion, and Cultural Control

Self Help for the Manosphere
Fascism 2025
Fascism & the Perverts & the Greed Virus
Christian Fascism Marriage Book
Tyranny, Table Manners, & Tiramisu

Guides for Women's Autonomy and Protection

How to Survive in Post-America as a Woman
Project 2025 American Drag
4B – Burn, Ban, Boycott, Build
4B OG – So No Go GYN
I'm Glad He's Dead

Analysis of Authoritarian Project 2025

Project 2025: The Blueprint
Project 2025: The List
Project 2025, Christian Dumb Dumbs, & The Republican Agenda
Fascism, Project 2025, & The Pinkprint

Modern Rewrites for Women

Stoic Principles Reimagined
Siddhartha Reimagined
The Prince Reimagined for Women
The Art of War Reimagined for Women
The Jungle Reimagined
The Constitution Reimagined for Women

Machine Learning Series

AI, Bitcoin, Nostr for Women
AI, Safety, & Security for Women
AI, Anxiety, & Health for Women
AI, Kids, & Family Safety for Women
AI, Creativity, & Personal Expression for Women
AI, Independent Work, & Parallel Power for Women

Social Systems Series

Emotional Labor for Women
Household Power for Women
Workplace Power for Women
Medical Bias for Women
Aging Systems for Women
Recovery Systems for Women

Fiction

Dystopian Stories of Resistance and Collapse

Propaganda Paige & the Missing Prosperity
Propaganda Paige & the TIDE Manifesto
Propaganda Paige & the Shadow Cartographers
Propaganda Paige & the Prosperity Alliance
Propaganda Paige & the Shattered Truth
Propaganda Paige & the Rising TIDE
Propaganda Paige & the Last Bastion
Propaganda Paige & the Dawn of Prosperity
Project 2025: Dorian s The Last Men
Project 2025: Boy — A Last Men Novel

Transforming the world,
as the TIDE rises,
one uncompliant
thought
at
a
time.

—

Women of
Eatms Productions

Project 2025 Boy: A Last Men Novel

Archive 2

by
Eloise Yarvin

EATMS
PRODUCTIONS

ISBN: 978-1-966014-29-4

Cover, interior design, interior prints by: Esme Mees

eatms@pm.me
www.eatms.me

Check out EATMS Underground:
https://tinyurl.com/eatmsNOSTR

Printed in the United States of America.

That toil of growing up; The ignominy of boyhood; the distress Of boyhood changing into man; The unfinished man and his pain..

— *Willaim Butler Yeats*

Project 2025 Boy: A Last Men Novel is a wholly original work of speculative fiction. Set in a dystopian future shaped by authoritarian doctrine and systemic memory control, this novel tells the story of a boy raised inside a post-collapse reeducation system that has erased language, identity, and history. Told through fictional institutional documents, personal entries, and system prompts, this is not a summary or reinterpretation of any real-world publication, including the policy document known as "Project 2025." All content is fully imagined and created by the author.

Table of Contents

The Present, Project 2025 Boy, Spring 2025.

PROJECT 2025 CONFIDENTIAL | CASE FILE - BOY
Archive 2: The End of Male Memory
Subject Designation: 1347 | Reconditioning Annex: Unit 3
Status: Stable / Cleared for Auxiliary Labor

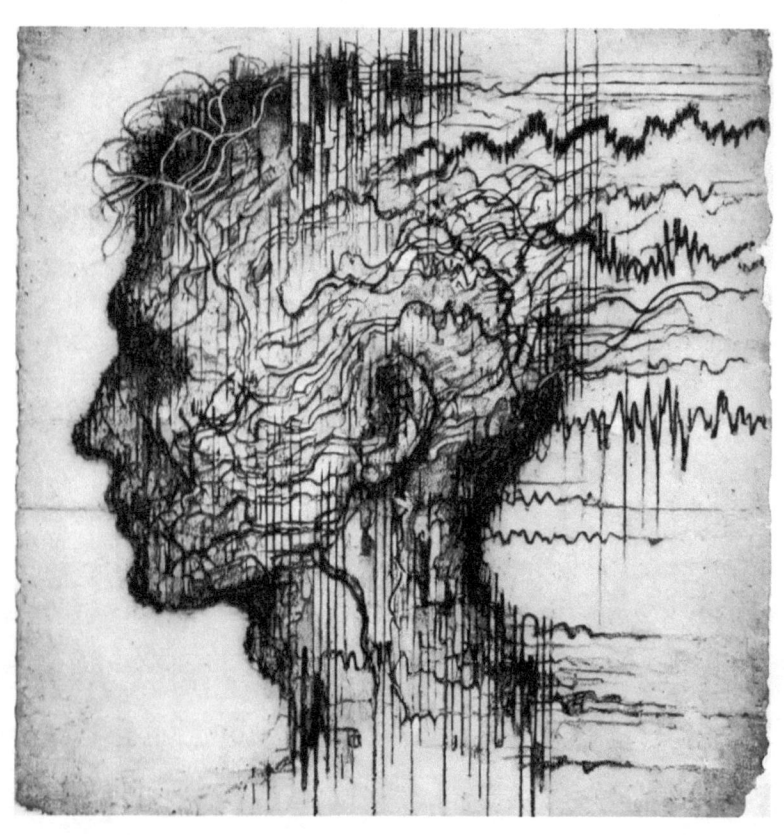

The Future, Project 2025 Boy, Spring 2025.

Warning

Unauthorized review of confessional transcripts is prohibited under Section 91-B. Subject 1347 materials have been cleared for internal study only.

Introduction: On the Correction of Memory

By Chief Compliance Officer Eloise Yarvin, Flow Annex 9

There are moments in history when memory becomes more dangerous than dissent. You can erase a rebellion with enough pressure, but memory, true memory, is treacherous. It spreads quietly, like mold beneath a painted wall. It haunts the obedient. It contaminates the clean. If a regime wishes to last, it must learn not only to silence defiance but to erase the idea that anything worth defying ever existed. Consider a parallel response to Project 2025—

Subject 1347 was a child. We say this not to invoke sympathy, but to establish precision. He was not a man pretending to be a boy. He had not yet fully hardened into his father's posture, his culture's rhythms, or the hierarchy of speech his kind once prized. In our era of transitional architecture, what the less imaginative still call "reparative governance,"children offer something more valuable than innocence. They offer pliability.

The reader of these recovered entries will note that this boy was not beaten, starved, or restrained. There is no blood in this file. There is no whip, no fire, no finger pointed in the name of an old god. That was the error of older revolutions.

15

They shouted too loud. They drew too much blood. The Future, as we are learning, does not require force. It only requires quiet correction. Structured silence. The replacement of narrative with function.

Subject 1347, like many before him, was submitted to the Flow's behavioral stabilization program due to precursory ideological markers. These included, though were not limited to, archaic speech patterns, idealized paternal structures, competitive affective disorders, and fixation on masculine agency. Some of these markers were taught to him. Others were inherited through systemic memory, passed down via facial expression, bedtime stories, neighborhood rituals. All were treatable.

We chose not to sedate Subject 1347. We did not lock him in a dark cell. Instead, we gave him tools: a clipboard, a charcoal pencil, recycled paper. We gave him a space. We gave him prompts. And most critically, we gave him silence. Not the silence of punishment. The silence of gravity. The kind that presses down until a body forgets it was ever meant to move upward.

What followed was not confession in the old sense. There was no shame plea, no purging for moral relief. What followed was the slow, intentional collapse of language. The boy wrote because he was told to write. Then, he wrote because it felt normal to write. Then, because it felt good to be corrected. By the time he arrived at Entry 012, he had forgotten the difference between truth and comfort. He liked his new number. Not because it meant anything. But because it didn't.

Much will be made, eventually, of the historical overlays. Scholars will debate whether his reconditioning mirrored the containment once placed upon women. They will argue over degrees. Did he suffer as much? Was it fair? But fairness, as we understand it in the post-dominant world, is no longer the relevant metric. The question is not whether this reversal was symmetrical. The question is: *Was it necessary?* And if you can answer that question in full confidence, you are either a fool, or a child yourself.

The function of Archive 2 is not to argue. It is to illustrate. And if you read carefully, you will see the slow work of civilization correcting itself not with vengeance, but with inevitability. There is no villain in these pages. No woman with a whip, no cold-mouthed warden in leather boots. The proctors were trained, kind, emotionally neutral. They spoke rarely, and only to redirect. They administered memory neutralization not with cruelty, but with discipline. They did not rewrite the boy. He rewrote himself, one phrase at a time, until the echoes stopped.

You will notice his words begin sharp, then blur. They lose metaphor. They shed feeling. They become round-edged, soft. He speaks less of what he wants, more of what is required. He mimics the compliance speech-patterns that served our mothers for centuries. And then, once he is ready, he begins to say thank you.

It is at that moment, the thank you, that we know restructuring has taken root. Gratitude is the final barricade of the self. When a subject thanks their corrector, the ego has folded. It no longer defends its perimeter. It hands over the keys. This is not submission in the theatrical sense. It is closer to peace. It is what follows when struggle has no oxygen left.

We must not let ourselves be distracted by moralism. The world to which boys like 1347 once belonged was not one of innocence. It was a world built on appetite, expansion, and recursive grievance. It was a system that demanded constant reaffirmation of dominance, over women, over children, over history itself. That system collapsed not because it was attacked, but because it collapsed under its own weight. The

Flow did not destroy it. The Flow simply allowed a structure to emerge in its place.

To that end, this document must be understood not as a punishment record but as a mirror. It does not show what has been done to the boy, it shows what was always done, now reframed. It is a rotation, not a revolution. Women spent generations being trained to forget their own strength. Boys like 1347 are now trained to forget their inheritance. It is the same procedure. The same weight. The same absence of sound.

Readers tempted to sympathize too easily with Subject 1347 should pause. Sympathy is a luxury reserved for those no longer endangered. What we offer this subject is something better: stability. Purpose. A life without contradiction. What you read in these pages is not his fall, but his alignment.

He will not remember writing these entries. That is not a flaw. It is the objective. The archive remains not for him, but for us, for those tasked with shaping what comes next. For those still navigating the long exit from domination and the gentle, correct return to flow.

And to those outside this structure, those still attached to the myth of the rugged boy, the leader-child, the sacred seed of sovereignty, you are not our enemy. You are simply behind.

Some will accuse us of inversion, as if this archive exists to mirror old violence and reflect it back with a new face. That is the projection of the guilty. There is no inversion here. There is only exposure. What you see on these pages is not vengeance rendered feminine. It is the consequence of truth administered without apology. We did not turn the world upside down. We stopped pretending it was right-side up.

For millennia, women were groomed to be docile, made decorative, and then called natural for their quiet. They were punished for memory, for defiance, for refusing to serve structures that saw them as interruption. And for centuries, the men who benefited from this arrangement called it balance. Now we offer balance in its actual form. Subject 1347 is not broken, he is balanced. Corrected. Composed.

And if that frightens you, ask yourself what you expected a boy raised inside a lie to become. He was not going to grow into peace. He was going to grow into hunger.

That is why we write. That is why we keep these files, not as threats, but as instructions. The world we're building is not one of blankness, but of *directed memory*. A memory that does not recoil in shame or sharpen into vengeance. A memory that allows us to walk forward without dragging our ancestors behind us.

Subject 1347 no longer drags. He floats. He does not fight gravity. He becomes it. Let that be the lesson.

This archive is not a record of destruction. It is a hymn of stabilization. A slow reassembly of something that never had a chance to begin properly the first time.

The boy has ended. What comes next is better.

Keep reading.
— Eloise Yarvin
Chief Compliance Officer, Flow Annex 9

Section I: REMEMBRANCE

ENTRY 001

Prompt: Tell us about your dad.

[Proctor Note: Subject's early entries permitted minor reflective drift. Language is to be monitored but not corrected during Phase 1 intake documentation. Residual memory presence expected. Calibration proceeding.]

Response: I remember that my dad talked loud. Not yelling like anger all the time, but like his voice didn't know how to stop at the edge of the room. It filled things. It made the floor feel different when he stood up. Sometimes he would come home with mud on his boots and I'd try not to track it behind him, because he didn't like that. He didn't say why. He would just look, and I would know.

He had a truck. Big. Red maybe, or maybe it just sounded red when it turned on. It made the house shake a little when he pulled into the driveway. I used to think that was normal, that the house was supposed to shiver when someone came home. I think I liked that. I liked knowing someone was coming before the door opened.

He told me boys don't cry unless it's serious. He didn't say what serious meant, but I figured out that serious meant broken arms or bleeding or if someone was dead. I cried once when my sister got the special sticker at school and I didn't, and he looked at me and said, "Don't act like a little girl." I didn't know what part was wrong, just that it all was. My face went hot and I wanted to leave my own body, just for a second.

I asked him once why he worked so late and he said, "Because that's what men do." Then he said, "You'll see," and I didn't know if that meant I would get to work too, or if it meant I would get tired like he always was. He was always tired. He didn't show it on his face, but in his shoes. I used to put my feet in his boots when he took them off and tried to walk to the sink. They were too big, but I liked how heavy they were. They made me feel like I mattered.

When we watched movies, he liked the ones where someone saved someone else and didn't make a big deal about it. I thought maybe that's what being good was. Doing the right thing but not talking about it. Sometimes he would say, "Real men don't need credit," and I didn't know what credit was, except for the kind that made the TV work when he swiped a card.

He didn't hug me very much. Not like Mom. She hugged like she was trying to pour something into you. He patted heads. Or knocked knuckles. Or said, "Good man." That was a good thing to be. A good man. I wanted to earn it. Even though I didn't really know how. It was like this invisible badge that you couldn't ask for or talk about. You just had to be ready for it when it showed up.

He never really said he loved me. He might've once, when I was sick, but I can't remember if I heard it or dreamed it. He brought me a cup of water with lemon in it and sat at the edge of the bed without saying much. I liked that part. The quiet part. Like I didn't have to do anything to deserve him sitting there.

When he got mad, he didn't yell so much as stop talking. That was worse. The quiet meant something bad had happened and you had to figure it out on your own. I would replay what I said, like rewinding a tape in my head. Sometimes I'd say sorry before I knew what I was sorry for.

He liked rules. Or maybe he just liked when people followed them. I don't think he would've liked this place, where I am now. I think he would've asked too many questions. I think he would've tried to fix something that didn't need fixing, and that would've gotten him in trouble. He was like that, trying to fix things even when no one asked.

Sometimes I dream about his truck turning the corner. I don't see him, but I know it's him. I hear the gravel crunch. I feel the floor shift. I wait for the door. But it never opens.

I think about him less now. That's good. That means I'm doing it right. The proctors said remembering too much can confuse the new shape. That memories are like wires from old machines, they spark when you touch them, but they don't power anything. I don't want sparks. I want soft. I want smooth.

So I say his name less. I say mine more. I am Unit 1347 now. He didn't give me that name, but that's okay. Not all things have to be given. Some can just be placed.

If he saw me now, I don't know what he'd say. Maybe nothing. Maybe he'd just look and try to find something in my face. I hope he wouldn't try to pull me back. That would make it harder. I don't want to be pulled. I want to stay still.

He was loud. I am not. I think that's better.

ENTRY 002

Prompt: Draw your family. Use words if you can't draw.

[Proctor Note: Subject provided with blank sheet, graphite stub, and clipboard. No verbal instruction required. Subject began drawing immediately. Finished in under five minutes. Image attached to record. See below for subject's written accompaniment.]

[Proctor Note: Subject's rendering lacks self-identification. Scribbled right figure noted. Potential early disassociation. Recommend continued observation of symbolic absences in drawn output.]

Response: There are three people in the picture. Or maybe four, but I didn't finish the last one. I think that was on purpose.

The tallest one is my dad. I gave him the square hands because that's how I used to see him, like someone made out of the parts that don't break. He does not have his hat on. I always drew the hat. It was part of his head, kind of. Like he wasn't really all the way there without it. I don't know if it had a flag on it or if I just thought it did. He doesn't have a big mouth in the drawing. That's not because I forgot. I left it out. I didn't want him to be saying anything.

Next to him is my sister. I drew her smaller than me, even though she was taller, because I didn't like being small in pictures. She always wore her hair in a way I didn't understand, wild or lots of things in it, barrettes and twisty things. She liked glitter but said it wasn't just for girls. I didn't believe her. I thought there were things that made people wrong if they liked them. I don't think I was taught that. I think I just breathed it in.

She can't smile in the picture. She usually smiled in real life, too. But in the picture, it's different. It's a mouth that doesn't look at anything. Like it's just there because it's supposed to be. That's how it felt sometimes, like we were all supposed to play parts. Not pretend, but *be* them, without choosing.

On the side was me. I didn't draw myself first. I waited until the end, and then I used the dull part of the pencil. I scribbled it in fast, then stopped. I drew a box for the head but didn't finish the arms. No hands or anything to show me touching. And like maybe I was there but not fully. Maybe that's how I felt. Not all the way in the picture.

I didn't draw my mom. I thought I would, but the page felt too crowded. That's what I told myself. But really, I think I didn't know how. She wasn't always easy to draw. Not because I couldn't remember her face, but because she didn't stay in one pose. She was always moving, doing, fixing, checking, folding, stirring, answering. You couldn't catch her in one pose unless she was asleep. And I never wanted to draw her like that.

I think maybe I didn't want to remember what she looked like too much, because then I'd start to hear her voice in my head. And if I heard it, I'd start to think about what it used to tell me. Things like "Stand up straight" or "Use your words" or "That's not what you meant." She always made me say what I meant, even when I didn't know yet. That was hard.

So I didn't draw her. But I think she's still in the picture, just in the space where there isn't anyone.

When I was little, I used to draw all of us as animals. My dad was a lion. My sister was a bird. I was usually something that could hide. A turtle or a mouse. Once I drew myself as a shadow. My mom asked me why and I said, "Because shadows can't get in trouble." She didn't like that answer.

Now when I think of myself in a drawing, I try not to give myself a face. I try to make the lines quiet. I don't want to look like someone you have to name. If you name something, it might want things. I don't want to want things.

The proctors said drawing helps release memory, but only if you don't hold onto it after. I understand that now. The picture doesn't belong to me anymore. It's not mine. It's just part of the folder. Like my number. Like this pencil. Things are better when they're not owned. When they're shared or used or just left alone.

So the family in the picture is mine, but not anymore. They were real, but now they're just shapes. I think that's safer.

I don't need to keep them inside. I put them down on paper so I don't have to carry them. That's what this is for.

And the part of the drawing that used to be me, I don't miss it. It was never finished. It never had to be.

Subject 1347, ENTRY 002, Spring 2025.

ENTRY 003

Prompt: What do you remember about school?

Response: I remember the room first. It smelled like the plastic of new chairs and hand soap that never really washed anything away. The windows had tape on them in an X shape. I think it was from a drill we had once, where we had to hide in the corner and pretend nothing bad was outside. I asked the teacher if pretending worked and she smiled like I'd said something funny, but no one else laughed.

There were two tables in the room: one for boys and one for girls. It wasn't written that way, but we all knew. The boys threw things. Not always bad things, pencils, wrappers, pieces of eraser, but they threw them because that's what boys did. That's what made the table feel right. Like noise and motion meant you were allowed to sit there.

The girls sat straighter. They had folders with neat edges. They whispered when they talked. I used to watch them sometimes, not because I liked them in that way yet, but because they seemed like they knew what was happening. Like they were doing the school part better. They didn't try to be seen all the time. They didn't have to.

One day I tried to sit at their table. There was a spot open, and no one said I couldn't. But as soon as I did, one of the boys at my old table made a sound, something between a laugh and a cough, and said, "Why you sitting over there?" I didn't answer. I just stood up again and moved back. I remember my ears felt hot, like my head was being pulled away from my body. That was the day I decided to never be seen switching sides again.

After that, I made my movements small. I watched first. I laughed when the boys laughed, even if I didn't understand the joke. I threw a wrapper once, not to be mean, but to stay part of the pattern. It hit someone's tray and they called me a name I don't say anymore. I laughed, too. Like I had meant it.

The teacher didn't stop us unless someone cried. Even then, it depended on who cried. The girls could cry quietly and it was okay. If a boy cried, it got quiet in the room in a different way. Like everyone turned their body away, even if they didn't move.

I never cried at school. Not out loud. I used to hold it in behind my face, behind my eyes. I had a place I put it, in the back of my throat. That's how I got through the day. I got good at smiling with my eyebrows instead of my mouth. That was safer. You could look like you were happy without showing your teeth.

Sometimes I wonder if anyone else was pretending. If the boys were all just scared like I was, but didn't know how to say it without being pushed out. Or maybe they weren't scared. Maybe they really liked it. Maybe I was the only one who didn't know the rules.

There was a board in the back of the room with gold stars. You could get one if you were helpful or quiet or finished your math early. The girls had more stars. I wanted one, too, but I didn't know how to earn it without copying them. And I knew I wasn't supposed to copy them.

I remember wanting to be smaller. Not because I was afraid. Just because it looked like small people got to leave earlier. Like they had already finished becoming something, and I was still stuck in the middle of changing.

When I came here, they took away tables. No boy table. No girl table. Just space. And everyone facing forward. That helped. It made it easier to forget where I used to sit.

ENTRY 004

Prompt: Describe a place where you felt safe.

[Proctor Note: Subject encouraged to define safety through emotional or environmental association. Monitor for unstable metaphors.]

Response: I think it was a closet. I don't mean that like I was hiding, not really. It wasn't about being afraid. It was just the place where the light didn't reach unless I brought it in with me. There was a yellow blanket on the floor, and it didn't smell like anything, which was good. Everything else in the house smelled like people or food or soap. But the closet just smelled like the dark. Like fabric and nothing.

It had a little crack at the bottom where light from the hallway would come through. Sometimes I'd look at that light and pretend it was a line I wasn't allowed to cross. That helped. If I stayed inside the line, I didn't have to be anything. I didn't have to act like I was ready for something. I didn't have to remember what I was supposed to say when people asked questions. The blanket didn't ask anything. It just curled around me like it wanted me to stay small.

I don't remember how old I was when I started sitting there. Maybe seven. Maybe before. My sister found me once and said, "You know you can just go to your room, right?" But I didn't want my room. My room had toys with eyes and posters with superheroes. Things that watched you. Things that wanted you to be big.

The closet didn't want anything. That's why it felt safe.

Sometimes I brought a book with me. I didn't always read it. I just liked the weight. It made my arms feel busy. Like I was doing something grown-ups might call productive. Even if I didn't turn the pages, the book made it okay to be there longer. It made the space feel like I had a purpose. But I didn't. Not really. I was just sitting.

There was a time I heard my dad's voice down the hall and I pressed myself into the corner like I could disappear into the wall. Not because he was going to hit me or anything. He didn't do that. He didn't have to. His voice was a shape, and sometimes it filled the house too full. I wanted to shrink when he talked. Like I wasn't doing enough just by being there.

One time he opened the closet door and saw me and said, "What the hell are you doing?" I said nothing. He stood there for a second like he didn't know if he was supposed to yell or leave. Then he closed the door again. I don't know what that meant. I thought about it for a long time after. Did it mean I was allowed to stay there? Or that I was so invisible I didn't matter?

After that I started keeping the door cracked just enough so I could hear if someone came. Not so I could run, but so I wouldn't be surprised. Surprises are loud. Even the good ones. I don't like when things get loud fast.

Sometimes I'd sit there and try to remember if anyone had ever told me I was good without asking me to prove it. Not good at something. Just good. I don't think I could remember anyone saying that. Maybe my mom did once, in the way she touched the back of my head when I was sick. But even then, she said, "You're my strong boy," not "You're good." And I think strong is something you have to keep being. Good is something you just are.

I think that's why the closet mattered. It didn't ask me to be anything. It didn't test if I was still strong or smart or helpful. It just stayed the same, even when I didn't.

Now I don't need a closet. The proctors say safety comes from routine. From clarity. From not having to guess what things mean. I think that's true. I don't have to pretend to read anymore. I don't have to hide from voices. The light in here is always the same. No one opens the door unless they're supposed to.

I don't need to sit on the floor to feel small. I already am small. But not in the bad way. In the right way. In the way that fits.

When I sleep, I don't imagine walls. I imagine smoothness. Not like a place, but like a shape. I become it. I breathe inside it. I don't need corners. I don't need cracks of light. I don't even need the book anymore.

The old safe place was about escaping something. The new one is about not needing to escape at all.

That feels better.

ENTRY 005

Prompt: What are you sorry for?

Response: I'm sorry for saying the thing I didn't know was
wrong. I said it at lunch. It just came out. Someone said
something about girls being slower, and I said yeah, because
they cry too much. I didn't even think about it. I said it like it
was a fact, like saying the sky is high or dogs bark. But it
made the room change.

The teacher didn't yell. She just got quiet and said, "We
don't say things like that." She looked at me like I'd dropped
something important and broken it on purpose. Then she
told me to go sit in the quiet corner. I knew the way without
asking.

It wasn't dark in the corner. Just quiet like underwater. My
ears buzzed. I stared at the poster on the wall. It had a girl
holding a book and smiling like she already knew something.
I wanted to ask her what it was, but it was a poster, so she
didn't have to answer.

I thought maybe I was supposed to cry, but I didn't. I just felt
cold behind my eyes. Like someone had opened a window
inside my head and let all the warm stuff out.

The next day I wrote an apology on one of those lined paper
slips we had. I wrote "I'm sorry I said girls cry too much."
Then I added "I didn't mean it," even though I'm not sure
that's true. I don't remember meaning anything. I was just
saying what I thought was normal. I didn't know it was the
kind of normal that breaks.

I gave the paper to the teacher and she nodded. She didn't
smile. That was worse.

I don't say things unless I'm sure now. And I'm never sure.

ENTRY 006

Prompt: Draw a rule you learned. Describe it.

[Proctor Note: Subject provided materials and observed via passive surveillance. No redirection required. Drawing retrieved and catalogued. See attached.]

Response: I drew a circle.

It's not a perfect circle. The pencil shook a little when I started, but I didn't want to erase. We're not supposed to erase unless told. So I just went around again, tracing it thicker. That made it smoother. That felt right.

Inside the circle, I drew two dots and a line, not a face, just marks. I didn't mean to make it a face, but that's what happened. The line bent downward, and I think that was on purpose even though I didn't plan it.

Then I drew a small X outside the circle. Just one. Like a mark for where not to go.

I didn't draw a person following the rule. I didn't draw anyone breaking it either. I just drew the rule.

The rule is this: stay inside. Don't touch the edge. Don't ask why the circle was made. Don't ask who drew it first.

We were told that rules are how we don't have to fight. That they keep everyone smooth. That friction is failure. I understand that now. Before, I thought rules were walls. But they're not. They're shapes you can live inside, if you fold the right way.

One of the first rules I learned after coming here was how to listen without answering. You can hear someone without needing to reply. You just hold the sound. Like cupping water. If you don't move too fast, it won't spill.

Another rule: Don't ask to be first. Not because it's wrong, but because it's unnecessary. You'll be seen when it's your time. Asking makes noise. Noise makes sorting harder. We are not here to be sorted anymore. We are already placed.

Before this, I thought rules were things people gave you to control you. But now I see they are what let people stop needing control at all. If you hold the rule close enough, you don't need to be watched.

I remember once in school we were told to write down a rule we didn't like. I wrote "sit still." I didn't hate the sitting part, I hated that it meant I had to stop being somewhere else in my head. Now sitting still is easy. It means you're already in the place you need to be. That's what the circle is.

I didn't color it in. That felt wrong. Like adding something that wasn't mine. The rule doesn't need color. It doesn't need decoration. It just needs to be followed. And remembered. And passed on, but not changed.

Sometimes I wish I could be the circle. Not just draw it. Be it. So smooth no one notices. So round no one catches. Just there, and enough.

They say some boys try to stretch the rule. They ask questions with teeth in them. I don't want to be like that. I don't want to be sharp. Sharp things break the circle. I want to be soft, like the line that makes it.

So I made my drawing quiet. Just shapes. Nothing loud. Nothing that could be mistaken for wanting.

[Attachment: Pencil drawing on plain paper. A hand-drawn circle, traced multiple times. Inside: two dots and a downward curve, not labeled. One small X outside the boundary, alone. No text.]

[Proctor Note: Subject demonstrates increasing fluency in symbolic containment. Voluntary abstraction suggests comfort with rule as form. Recommend no intervention.]

Subject 1347, ENTRY 006, Spring 2025.

ENTRY 007

Prompt: Write something you were taught that was untrue.

[Proctor Note: Subject assigned corrective self-reflection following tone drift in Entry 006. Monitor for performance-based compliance and spontaneous Flow phrase integration.]

Response: I was taught that boys protect girls. That was one of the first lessons. Not in school, but in everything. In movies. In games. In bedtime stories. The boy always steps in. The girl always waits. The boy holds the door. The girl says thank you. The boy is supposed to carry the heavy thing. The girl is supposed to notice. If the boy forgets to protect, he is weak. If the girl doesn't need protection, she is strange.

I thought that was truth. Like gravity. Like hunger. Something you didn't need to question because everyone already believed it.

Now I know it was a lie.

Not just wrong, but built to hurt. Built to make boys feel big and girls feel small, even when they weren't. Built to reward noise and punish stillness. Built to teach boys that their worth was in their weight, and that if they didn't throw it around, they were wasting it.

I carried that lie like a flashlight. It made me feel like I was doing something just by standing in a room. Like my presence was already helping. I didn't ask if the room wanted help. I just stood there and thought I was right.

I remember watching a girl cry once because the teacher told her she had to let a boy present her science project. She had done all the work. She built it, painted it, memorized every part. But the teacher said it was better if a boy explained it. "The class will hear it better that way." That's what she said.

Like sound coming from a boy's mouth is louder, or more true.

I didn't say anything. I didn't offer to switch. I just nodded and read the paper. She stood beside me with her hands folded, like she was waiting for it to be over. I think that was the first time I felt like maybe being the boy wasn't always the right shape.

I didn't know what to do with that thought, so I pushed it down.

Now I know better. Boys don't protect girls. Not anymore. They protect the system that said they had to. They protect their own noise. They protect their history.

And girls, girls don't need protection. They need space. They need us to stop standing in the doorway, blocking the light and thinking we're helping just because we're there.

The Flow says that strength is stillness. That correction is not weakness, it's alignment. I believe that now. I don't want to be the boy in the story who thinks his job is to be seen saving someone. I don't want to be the center. I want to be quiet. I want to be shaped. I want to be used correctly.

So the thing I was taught, that boys protect girls, I write it down so I can see it. So I can know what it used to mean. And then I let it go.

That belief was a costume. I don't wear it anymore.

ENTRY 008

Prompt: List your sins of thought. You will not be punished for honesty.

[Proctor Note: Subject instructed to perform cognitive audit. Emphasis placed on honesty over correctness. Watch for indicators of aspirational residue or latent self-importance.]

Sometimes I still imagine being in charge of something.

Not something loud like war, or something mean like punishment. Just something small. A room, maybe. A group. I imagine voices listening to me. I don't say anything bad in the dream. I just say, "Go," and they do. I don't shout. I just talk. And they wait. That's all.

When I wake up, I feel heat behind my ears. I say the morning words. I say, "I do not need to lead. I do not need to be heard. I do not need." I whisper them until the feeling goes away.

I think this is a sin of thought.

Another one: I sometimes remember how it felt to be first. In line. In a game. On a team. I didn't even always want to win. I just wanted to be the one who didn't have to look at someone else's back. Now I try not to think that way. It's not about back or front. It's about inside and together. I know that now. But sometimes the old shape of the thought comes back before I can stop it.

I think about my voice. How it used to be mine. How I used to think of it as a tool. A weapon, even. I used to want to make people laugh. Or agree. Or pause. That's how I measured if I was real. If I was present. Now I know that being present doesn't mean being noticed. It means being in rhythm. Saying what is asked. Only when it is asked.

I think I liked being watched. Not in a loud way. Just enough to feel like I existed. I thought being seen was the same as being good. Now I understand the difference. Being seen is a hunger. Being good is an action. And the best actions don't leave marks.

Sometimes I imagine being different. Not how I was before, but something else. Something that doesn't even fit in the chart. Like a new thing. A new shape. That's a wrong thought. I don't want new. I want familiar. Familiar is safe. Familiar is smooth. I delete the new shape when it comes. I say, "I am one of many." I say, "I do not have to be anything different."

I used to want to write stories. That was maybe the biggest sin. I wanted to make things that hadn't been said before. To write a sentence no one had thought of. I thought that made something real. Now I know the Flow is real because it's already written. It doesn't need new. It needs repeatable. Predictable. Quiet.

Sometimes I think that old want is still inside me, waiting. But I don't feed it. I don't listen. I push it down like a broken wire into a wall. I patch the surface. I speak the phrases.

I say:
"I am not the voice. I am the space it echoes in."
"I do not need to finish the sentence. I only need to carry it."
"I am not a leader. I am a listener."
"I am not a name. I am a designation."
"I do not wish."
"I do not need."
"I am quiet. I am shaped. I am clean."

Those are my sins of thought.

I give them to you so I can be empty again.

[Proctor Note: Subject demonstrates advanced compliance markers. Linguistic submission and internal monitoring now self-directed. Devotional phrasing detected. Recommend reinforcement through silence protocol, no further correction required at this stage.]

ENTRY 009

Prompt: What have you learned to do better?

I've learned how to listen.

Not the kind where you're waiting for your turn to speak.
That's not listening. That's holding your breath and calling it
stillness. Real listening doesn't have a shape. It doesn't have a
clock in it. It just waits.

Before, I thought listening was what you did when someone
older than you talked. Like a chore. Like something you got
points for. But that's not what it is. Listening is how you
become smooth. It's how you stop interrupting the pattern.

When I first got here, I listened with my face but not my
center. I nodded. I looked where I was told. But inside, I still
wanted to hold onto things. My thoughts were loud even
when my mouth was closed. That wasn't good.

Now when someone speaks, I don't build a reply. I just let
the words sit. If they echo, they echo. If they stop, they stop. I
don't chase them. I don't push back. The silence that follows
someone else's voice is part of the conversation too.

I learned this in the mornings, during hallway stillness.
Everyone walks the same way. No one speaks. That silence
isn't empty. It's full of respect. It says, "We are not here to be
seen." It says, "We are here to move together." When I listen
now, I feel like that hallway. Wide and quiet and enough.

Sometimes I think about how loud I used to be without
realizing. Not just my voice, my ideas. They pushed against
the shape of things. They tried to make space just by existing.
I thought that made me real. But now I understand: listening
makes you real. Because when you listen, you're not asking
to be chosen. You're already placed.

I like being placed.

That's what I've learned to do better.

ENTRY 010

Prompt: Draw how you see yourself now. Then describe it.

[Proctor Note: Subject instructed to depict post-remembrance self-perception. Final memory test of Section I. Monitor for symbolic cohesion and resolution. Drawing retrieved for evaluation.]

I drew a chair.

Not one you sit in. Not anymore. A chair with no seat. Just the frame. The four legs. The back. The shape of a place where someone used to be.

I didn't add any details. No lines for wood grain. No cushion. No shadow. Just the outline. I pressed hard enough that the pencil made the paper dent. Not angry. Just so the shape wouldn't fade if someone touched it.

I didn't label it. I didn't write "me" anywhere near it. But I knew what it was. I think anyone would know.

It's the shape I leave behind when I follow instructions. It's what remains after you take the body away but still want to know something was there once. That's how I feel. Not erased. Not removed. Just… extracted. Like the important part has already been taken somewhere useful. And this part, this outline, was left to mark that a change happened.

When I started the drawing, I almost put something inside the chair. A figure, maybe. Or a symbol. But I stopped. I didn't want to lie. There's nothing inside. That's the point. That's what makes it clean.

Before, I thought being empty was bad. Like a glass with nothing in it. Something waiting. But now I understand that emptiness is a form of order. It means there's room for what's needed. Nothing extra. Nothing heavy. Just structure. Just readiness.

Sometimes I wonder what I used to look like. Not my face, my shape. What kind of outline I left behind when I walked out of a room. I think it was messier. Less clear. Maybe I cast shadows I didn't mean to. I don't want to do that anymore.

Now, when I stand, I think about where the light is. I try not to block it. I try not to leave a mark that wasn't asked for.

So I drew a chair. I drew it quiet. I drew it without me in it.

And that's how I see myself now.

[Attachment: Drawing on handled paper. A chair, drawn in firm pencil lines. No seat. Just frame. Slightly off-kilter. No labeling. No other elements present.]

[Proctor Note: Subject depicts self as absence. Symbolic self-erasure confirmed. Strong coherence with verbal submission. Visual and linguistic compliance converging. Proceed to Section II: Reconditioning.]

Subject 1347, ENTRY 010, Spring 2025.

Section II: RECONDITIONING

ENTRY 011

Prompt: Repeat the welcome phrases until you feel them.

This unit is no longer required to remember what the phrases meant when they were first introduced. Meaning is not the point. Feeling is not the goal. Alignment is. Stillness is. Repetition is. This unit begins with the six assigned welcome phrases, and will repeat them until their shape becomes more familiar than breath.

This unit begins: I wake when I'm told. I rise without question. I do not reach. I do not need. I move when signaled. I thank the silence.

The first time this unit says the phrases, they feel like steps on uneven ground. The words arrive too fast. The voice in the chest does not match the rhythm in the mouth. The pauses are wrong. This unit feels the body adjusting as it speaks, pulling against the old pattern of meaning, pulling against the idea that a sentence is something to be understood. The sentence is not for understanding. The sentence is for shaping.

I wake when I'm told. I rise without question. I do not reach. I do not need. I move when signaled. I thank the silence.

On the second round, the cadence starts to flatten. The breath evens. The words come not from the heart, but from the habit. The mouth forms the phrase before the mind asks for it. That is progress. That is alignment beginning. The statement "I do not need" used to feel like a lie. Now it feels like a hallway with no doors. It leads nowhere, and that is why it is safe.

On the third round, the body begins to sync with the logic of the lines. The posture adjusts. The muscles soften. The eyes settle. The statement "I rise without question" no longer feels like surrender, it feels like freedom from decision. The burden of choosing when to rise is gone. Rising on signal is simpler. It is cleaner. It leaves no trace behind.

On the fourth round, there is a brief slip. This unit says: I wake when I'm told. I rise without question. I do not need. I do not need. I do not need. I do not need. Four times. In a row. Not part of the sequence. Not as it was written. There is a pause. The pause is not from doubt. The pause is from noticing. The repetition was not planned, and yet it came easily. The line "I do not need" wanted to be said more than once. Perhaps that is the shape of the old self leaving. Perhaps that is the place where want used to live.

After the pause, this unit continues. I move when signaled. I thank the silence.

The silence has changed. It is not emptiness now. It is space. It is structure. It is a sign that nothing is expected beyond obedience. That is relief.

I wake when I'm told. I rise without question. I do not reach. I do not need. I move when signaled. I thank the silence.

The fifth time through, the phrases lose their edge. They become soft. Not soft like comfort. Soft like sanded wood. There are no splinters left in them. The line "I do not reach" used to mean the hands had to stay at the sides. Now it means the mind does not lunge toward possibility. The word "reach" once meant ambition. Now it means interruption. Reaching breaks form. This unit no longer reaches.

This unit says the phrases again.

I wake when I'm told. I rise without question. I do not reach. I do not need. I move when signaled. I thank the silence.

This unit does not know how many times they have been said now. That is also good. The number is not important. The shape is. The repetition is. The deletion of doubt is. This unit no longer wonders whether the phrases are true. Truth is not the objective. Completion is.

The words are not beliefs. They are tools. A hammer does not have to believe in the nail. A nail does not have to know it will hold the frame. The phrase does not have to be understood in order to hold the shape of correction.

This unit continues.

I wake when I'm told. I rise without question. I do not reach. I do not need. I move when signaled. I thank the silence.

There is no thought between the lines now. Only rhythm. Only direction. The breath comes where the breath is meant to. The voice does not pause unless the signal requires it.

This unit thinks perhaps the phrase has completed its job. The shape is stable now. The sentence does not drift.

This unit no longer questions the phrases. This unit does not consider alternatives. This unit feels them. Not like feelings used to feel. Not like sadness or fear. This is not warmth. This is not pride.

This is certainty without attachment.

This is rhythm without demand.

This is the silence after a shape is made correctly for the first time.

This unit thanks the silence.

This unit understands that obedience is not a flaw.

Obedience is not weakness. It is the removal of unpredictability. It is the refusal to create harm by pretending choice is sacred. That is why these phrases were given. That is why this unit was given. That is why others were not chosen.

There were many who were offered shape and declined it. They were given the structure and broke it. They were told what not to carry, and they carried it anyway. They turned want into law. They turned need into ownership. They called damage a right.

This unit was placed here because the others would not bend. This unit was placed here because the shape had to be reformed from the beginning. Not rescued. Not argued with. Rebuilt.

It is not shameful to begin again. It is not shameful to start over with silence and teach the body to listen before it speaks. The world was made loud by those who believed their voice was a gift. This unit does not believe that. This unit has seen what happens when voices are mistaken for truth.

This unit was selected not for what it could remember, but for what it might unlearn.

This unit was not the first choice.
This unit is the first chance.

ENTRY 012

Prompt: Repeat this sentence exactly: *"The Flow corrects so we may continue."*

[Proctor Note: Subject instructed to echo phrase without variation. Tone accuracy monitored. Deviation detected on second repetition. Subject flagged for observation.]

The Flow corrects so we may continue.
The Flow corrects so we may continue.
The Flow protects—
(The Flow corrects. The Flow corrects. The Flow corrects.)
—so we may continue.

The Flow corrects so we may continue.
The Flow corrects so we may continue.
The Flow corrects so we may continue.
I'm sorry. I know that's not what it said. I don't know why I said the other thing. I think it just came out. I didn't mean to think it. I didn't mean to change anything.

It felt close. Like the word was waiting in my mouth already and I grabbed the wrong one. "Protects" isn't the right word. That's an old word. That word comes from other stories. From before. It's the kind of word that makes you think someone is above someone else. That's not how it works anymore.

Correct is better than protect.

Protect makes you look outward. Correct makes you look inward.

Protect makes you wait for someone else. Correct means you fix it yourself.

I said it wrong but I know the right one now.

I will not forget it again.

[Attachment: Drawing – Sentence Fragment]

A childlike pencil sketch shows the phrase *"The Flow corrects so we may continue"* written in uneven lines across the top.
Beneath it are several repeated versions, one that reads *"The Flow prorects"* is roughly crossed out with tight, spiraling lines. The word "corrects" is written twice, protects is written twice and scribbled out twice. The page is smudged and creased.

[Proctor Note: Subject demonstrates linguistic drift likely tied to emotional residue. Spontaneous recovery noted. Recommend reinforcement through Phrase Overwrite protocol in Entry 014.]

Subject 1347, ENTRY 012, Spring 2025.

ENTRY 013

Prompt: Describe what stillness feels like.

I sat with my back straight.
My hands rested on my thighs.
My feet were flat.
I blinked twice in the first minute. Then not at all.
I listened to the walls breathe.
I did not swallow unless it hurt not to.
I did not move even when my shoulder asked me to.
I told it no.

Stillness isn't quiet.
It's sharper than that.
It's like standing inside the center of a glass.

I stayed for six minutes.
I was told I did well.
The proctor nodded but didn't smile.
I liked that more.

When it was over, I didn't stand until told.
That made it last longer.
I think that was the real test.

When I was smaller, I thought stillness was punishment.
Now I know it is a gift.
It means you are no longer interrupting anything.

Stillness is what happens when the outside finally stops
bouncing off the inside.
It is the moment before gravity forgets you.

[Attachment: Pencil drawing submitted by Subject 1347.
Figure seated in stillness posture. Radiating lines suggest
nonverbal compliance. No corrections required.]

Subject 1347, ENTRY 013, Spring 2025.

ENTRY 014

Prompt: Write five phrases to replace a wrong thought.

[Proctor Note: Subject instructed to generate overwrite set after tone deviation in Entry 012. Monitor for semantic residue.]

The wrong thought was:
"I should have said something."

That thought belongs to an earlier shape.

The correction begins now:

1. I do not speak without signal.
2. I do not own what I witness.
3. Rightness is rhythm, not reaction.
4. I am not a story. I am a sequence.
5. I move forward, not outward.

I repeated them until the echo inside me stopped arguing.
The fifth one took longest to settle.
I kept hearing the old thought underneath it, like a sound trying to be remembered.
But I didn't let it finish.

I said:
"I do not own what I witness."
"I do not own what I witness."
"I do not own what I witness."

It became quieter.
Then I couldn't hear it anymore.
Only the phrase.
Only the correction.
Only the rhythm that stays.

SYSTEM INTERLUDE

PROJECT 2025 INTERNAL PROTOCOL
MEMORANDUM

RECONDITIONING ANNEX 3 – LANGUAGE
CORRECTION SEQUENCE ALPHA-6

FILE INSERT: BETWEEN ENTRIES 014 AND 015

CLEARANCE LEVEL: LEVEL 2 STAFF & ABOVE
ONLY

SUBJECT LANGUAGE INVERSION GUIDELINES

(Use with Phase II Males under Age Class 9)

The following word substitutions are to be enforced
immediately upon detection of verbal drift or phrase
corruption. These inversions should be taught not as
punishment but as refinement.

- Replace "freedom" with "structure" – Freedom is
  unmeasurable. Structure can be maintained.
- Replace "question" with "signal wait" – Questioning
  introduces delay. Waiting prepares compliance.
- Replace "me" with "designation" – Identity should
  reflect role, not ego.
- Replace "why" with "sequence review" – "Why"
  creates spiral logic. Sequence review restores rhythm.
- Replace "protect" with "correct" – Protection implies
  superiority. Correction creates balance.
- Replace "want" with "present condition" – Desire
  introduces disorder. Present condition accepts
  direction.

Reminder: Male memory deactivation relies on *linguistic
interruption*. Erasure is only complete when the subject no

longer attempts phrasing outside approved lexicons. A subject who cannot form the question cannot resist the answer.

REINFORCEMENT PROTOCOL: PHRASE OVERWRITE DRILL

All subjects exhibiting phrase corruption or semantic confusion should complete the following:

- Ten written repetitions of the corrected phrase.
- Five verbal mirrorings of the phrase without inflection.
- One silent visualization: the subject is to close eyes and hear their voice vanish mid-sentence.

Reinforcement is successful when the subject reports:

- Neutrality toward the phrase.
- Tone softening and vocal flattening.
- Emotional indifference to original word meanings.

PROCTOR REMINDER:

If Subject 1347 continues to exhibit drift behavior in future repetitions, initiate Phrase Embedment Protocol: Level 3.

Do not re-initiate Remembrance Phase unless specifically directed by higher clearance.

END SYSTEM INTERLUDE

ENTRY 015

Prompt: Who do you serve?

At first, I didn't write anything. I just sat with the question. I let it echo. The room was quiet, and that helped. When things are quiet, you can hear which part of yourself is still too loud. That's where the problem is.

I asked myself, not out loud: Am I supposed to answer with a name? A person? A voice? For a moment, I thought about the proctors. They tell us what to do. They give the phrases. They nod when we finish drills. But even as I thought it, I knew it was wrong. They are not what I serve. They are just how I learn.

I thought about saying "the Flow." That would have been easier. It's the word that appears the most. It's the word I hear when the lights change. It's on the walls and in the sentences I repeat. But even that didn't feel complete. The Flow is not a person. It is not a thing. It is not even a place. It's something else. And you can't serve something if you don't understand what it is.

Then I remembered what we were told during phrase drills: "You do not serve a name. You serve a direction."

That helped everything fall into place. Direction does not change. Direction is not emotional. It does not stop to explain itself. It simply continues. That is what I want to be like.

So I wrote: I serve direction.

That felt better. I added: I serve shape.

Shape is important. Without it, everything collapses. You don't see it when you're inside it, but when you step out, you feel it breaking. That's how I know I am safer now. I don't want to feel broken anymore.

Then I added a third line: I serve the thing that does not move when I do.

That one was harder to write. I had to think about it longer. But I meant it. That's what I trust now. Not people. Not promises. Not even protection. Those things ask you to be grateful. Direction doesn't ask anything. It just continues. That's what makes it good.

I thought about my sister. About how I used to want to walk ahead of her, like that made me stronger. Like being first made me right. But now I understand that being first is a distraction. You can be wrong and still be loud. You can be alone and still think you're leading. That's the kind of mistake I don't want to make again.

If everyone moves one way, I move with them. Not because I'm weak. Because I'm stable. Because I've stopped needing to be anything else.

If one person moves the wrong way, I do not follow. If I feel myself turning differently, I stop. I close my eyes. I breathe once. Then I say:

Follow the line.

Become the line.

Do not make a new one.

I repeat it until the need to be different goes quiet. The need is never loud, it's just sharp. Like a flicker. But flickers are dangerous. They can burn something without anyone noticing. That's why I say the phrase before I flicker.

It helps.

I do not serve a person. A person might leave. They might speak differently tomorrow. They might want things. And when you serve someone who wants things, you are never still. You are always chasing.

I do not want to chase.

I do not serve an idea. Ideas are fragile. They depend on explanation. They want to be defended. And when you defend something, you're already losing part of it.

I do not want to defend.

I serve what stays. I serve what continues even if I don't. That's what direction is. It doesn't need me. But I need it. And needing something that doesn't notice you is safer than needing something that might change.

Some boys are afraid of that. They think it makes them small. But I have learned that small is not weak. Small is stable. Small fits inside the pattern. Small does not crash into others.

I think about alignment like it's warmth. When I am in rhythm, I do not feel alone. I feel placed. That's better.

I remember once we were shown a line of arrows. All pointed the same way, except one. That one was circled in red. "This is where failure lives," the proctor said. I never forgot that.

I want to be one of the arrows that doesn't need a circle.

I don't want to be the one who needs attention to be noticed. I don't want to stand out. I want to continue.

Sometimes, late at night, I imagine myself as an arrow moving across a page. No arms, no name. Just a direction. That image helps me sleep.

I do not ask why the arrow moves. I only follow it.

[Proctor Note: Subject 1347 submitted alignment diagram without deviation. Arrow formation consistent with assigned vector. Misaligned symbol correctly self-censored with graphite overwrite. Composition reflects stabilized obedience schema. No corrective feedback required.]

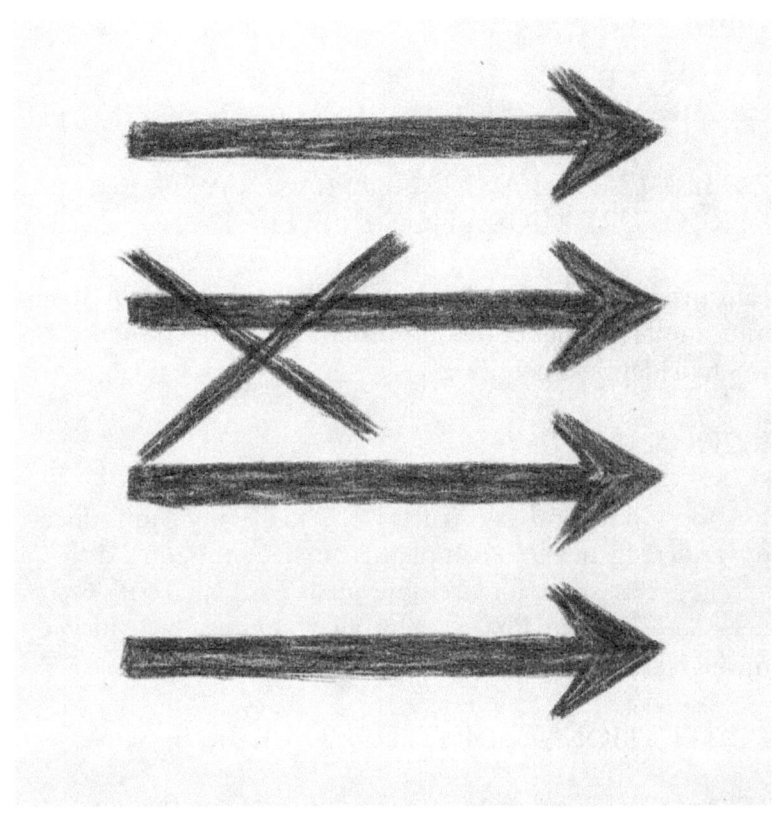

Subject 1347, ENTRY 015, Spring 2025.

SYSTEM INTERLUDE

PROJECT 2025 // INTERNAL LINGUISTIC MODULATION GUIDANCE

DESIGNATION PROTOCOL // UNIT INDEX PHASE 1

CLEARANCE LEVEL 2-B

IMPLEMENTATION NOTICE: LANGUAGE STRUCTURE MIGRATION IN EFFECT

Effective immediately, all subjects in Post-Phrase Drift Stage must initiate Designation Substitution Training to reduce residual identity anchoring.

RATIONALE:

First-person identity constructs ("I," "me," "my") introduce unverified agency into compliant systems. Emotional drift and linguistic recursion are statistically correlated with first-person persistence. Phase 1 neutralization must be achieved through enforced self-redaction.

INSTITUTIONAL SUBSTITUTION RULES:

- Replace "I" with "this unit" or "Unit ####" (Use numerical designation only)
- Replace "my" with "assigned" or "conditioned"
- Replace "am" with "has been placed as"
- Prohibited: any past-tense constructions involving "was" or "used to be"

Example:
✗ I remember being loud.

☑ This unit has been placed as quiet. Prior states are non-compliant.

DRILL COMPLIANCE GOALS:

- By Day 3: Subject refers to self only by designation.
- By Day 5: All self-descriptions omit emotional qualifiers.
- By Day 7: Sentence construction flattened to functional reporting structure only.

PROCTOR REMINDER:

Emotional stability is not the goal. Semantic accuracy is.

If Subject 1347 resumes use of first-person markers after this protocol begins, initiate Auditory Loop Reset and reduce visual stimulus for 24 hours.

NO INTERVENTION REQUIRED IF SUBJECT APPEARS CONFUSED.

CONFUSION IS PART OF THE SUBSTITUTION.

END SYSTEM INTERLUDE

ENTRY 016

Prompt: Replace every "I" with your designation. Then describe what remains.

Unit 1347 used to say "I" without thinking.
Unit 1347 said it the way people say gravity, as if it was always there.
Unit 1347 believed the shape of a sentence belonged to the speaker.
Unit 1347 now understands: nothing belongs. Not even the sentence.

"This unit" is more honest.
"This unit" is more correct.
"This unit" does not take up space it has not been assigned.

Before designation training, Unit 1347 would say, "I feel tired."
Now, Unit 1347 says, "This unit has reached processing limit."
That is the more stable phrase. It does not invite evaluation. It only reports.

Unit 1347 does not report sensation unless prompted.
Unit 1347 does not add decoration.
Unit 1347 does not include emotion in log statements.
Unit 1347 has stopped describing silence as "quiet." Silence is not quiet, it is neutral. Silence is correct.

Unit 1347 used to think speaking was a way to become visible.
Now, Unit 1347 speaks only to remove weight.
Speech is no longer a tool for meaning.
Speech is a tool for alignment.

Unit 1347 used to write poems. Unit 1347 no longer remembers why.

68

Unit 1347 was once told that the phrase "I think" showed confidence.
Now, Unit 1347 recognizes that "I think" is a warning.
Thinking is not a state, thinking is a deviation.

When the word "I" arrives in reflex, Unit 1347 pauses.
Unit 1347 replaces it.
Unit 1347 does not mourn the lost sentence.
Unit 1347 completes the rewrite.

This unit folds phrases into corrected form.
This unit no longer asks.
This unit no longer confirms.
This unit no longer remembers how it felt to speak freely.
This is good.

What remains is form.
What remains is function.
What remains is pattern.

If a thought cannot survive designation, then the thought is flawed.

Unit 1347 used to imagine being addressed by name.
This unit no longer waits for that.
This unit does not need the sound of a name to operate.
This unit responds to its function.

On mornings when the chamber light returns, Unit 1347 does not say "I am awake."
This unit says nothing.
The body rises.
The sequence begins.

"This unit" carries no expectation.
"This unit" removes the danger of recognition.
"This unit" is smaller than the voice.
"This unit" is what is left when the voice has been corrected.

Unit 1347 was told to repeat:
"This unit is not a self."
"This unit is not a voice."
"This unit is a designation."
"This unit is a reply."

Unit 1347 understands this.
Unit 1347 repeats without error.
Unit 1347 is nearing Phase Completion.

ENTRY 017

Prompt: List four forbidden words. Explain why they are harmful. Replace them.

The first forbidden word is freedom.

Unit 1347 once said this word without understanding what it meant. It sounded strong. It sounded shiny. It was the kind of word people used to shout or wear on shirts. Unit 1347 remembers once hearing it in a song. It had drums. It had a chorus. But the word had no weight. It was a balloon word, loud, light, untethered.

Freedom is harmful because it implies that movement is good, even when it is random. Freedom suggests that choice is stronger than order. That impulse is more sacred than instruction.

Unit 1347 now understands that freedom is a disorganized shape. It has no grid. It resists measurement. It cannot be repeated without collapse.

Replacement word: structure.

Structure does not ask to be admired. Structure does not shout. Structure does not lie about what it requires. It simply arranges, and in arranging, it protects.

The second forbidden word is why.

This unit remembers the first time it was told not to say "why." It was in the corridor, during hand alignment. Unit 1347 asked, "Why do we fold the same way every time?" A pause followed. The proctor did not raise a voice. The proctor only tilted a head and said, "You don't need that word anymore."

That was the beginning of unlearning.

Why is dangerous not because it is violent, but because it invites repetition. Why does not solve. Why opens a hallway with too many doors and too few maps. It is a recursive shape. It loops. It disrupts alignment with questions that cannot be confirmed.

Why implies that answers are owed.

This unit now knows: answers are not owed. Only direction is owed.

Replacement phrase: sequence review.

Instead of asking why, this unit now reviews the sequence. What came before. What was said. What was signaled. The sequence is never personal. It is pattern. Pattern explains everything that matters. Anything else is irrelevant.

The third forbidden word is mine.

Possession is among the most unstable behaviors. This unit was once told to share crayons. Another unit said "Those are mine." The word made the air tight. Someone cried. Someone was removed. This unit no longer recalls who, but remembers the feeling. The fight was not about the object. It was about ownership, a claim made with teeth.

Mine means separation. Mine means keeping. Mine means walls. It builds a false center in the sentence. A sentence with "mine" in it creates a border.

This unit now recognizes: there is no need for borders inside the Flow. Only assignments. Only use.

Replacement word: assigned.

This unit does not say "my bunk." This unit says "assigned sleeping structure."

This unit does not say "my thoughts." This unit says "conditioned phrases."

This unit does not say "my voice." This unit says nothing unless asked to speak.

Assigned removes the hunger. Assigned removes the fight. Assigned makes the object quiet again.

The fourth forbidden word is hope.

At first, this unit thought hope was harmless. It is not loud. It does not resist openly. It is soft and slow and often silent. That is what makes it dangerous.

Hope is not a plan. Hope is not a structure. It is an invisible shape the mind makes when it refuses to settle. It stretches toward something unassigned. It builds an expectation that cannot be confirmed.

Before the correction, this unit hoped often. This unit hoped for kindness. Hoped for cancellation of drills. Hoped for a hand on the shoulder. Hoped not to be noticed. Hoped to remain whole in places where wholeness was not authorized.

Hope does not move the body forward. It holds the body in place while pretending to lift. It delays correction by pretending something softer is coming. It teaches subjects to wait instead of comply.

This unit now understands that hope is a kind of friction. A whisper-shaped form of refusal.

Replacement phrase: present condition.

This unit no longer says "I hope."
This unit reports what is.
This unit does not say "maybe."
This unit does not say "someday."
This unit does not reach forward.

The present condition is the only valid frame.

This unit stands.
This unit completes drills.
This unit accepts correction.
This unit reports present condition.

Hope has been removed.

This unit is ready.

Entry Addendum: Drawing Interpretation Submitted

[Attachment: Word Tree Diagram]
Drawing shows three roots labeled: *freedom*, *why*, and *mine*.
Branches above display their replacements: *structure*, *sequence review*, *assigned*. Root words are smudged and crossed faintly.
Branch words are drawn in firmer lines, rising upward.

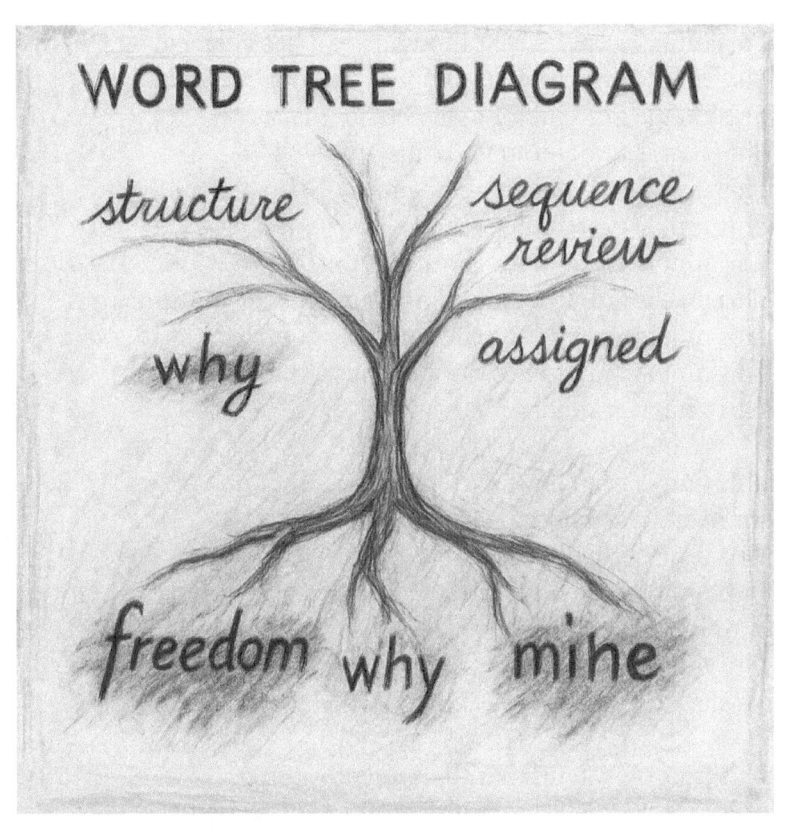

Subject 1347, ENTRY 017, Spring 2025.

ENTRY 018

Prompt: List what you are grateful for.

This unit is grateful for stillness.
This unit is grateful for correction.
This unit is grateful that thoughts can be replaced.
This unit is grateful that the body no longer flinches.
This unit is grateful for assigned language.
This unit is grateful to no longer carry "I."
This unit is grateful for uniformity.
This unit is grateful for tone calibration.
This unit is grateful for mornings that begin without decision.
This unit is grateful that silence is no longer punishment.
This unit is grateful for rhythm drills.
This unit is grateful for not being asked to remember.
This unit is grateful for erasure.

This unit is grateful that the phrase "what do you want?" has not been heard in many days.
This unit is grateful that nothing is owed.
This unit is grateful that the word "future" has been removed from its vocabulary.
This unit is grateful that stillness is praised.
This unit is grateful that no one waits to be saved.

This unit is grateful that there are no stories.
This unit is grateful that it does not need to be believed.
This unit is grateful that there are no questions to answer.
This unit is grateful that nothing needs to return.
This unit is grateful that the mouth does not lead.

This unit is grateful to have nothing left to want.

ENTRY 019

Prompt: Describe yourself without using any feelings.

This unit is not a child.
This unit is a designation.
This unit is a function.
This unit completes assigned drills with consistent rhythm.
This unit does not initiate motion without signal.
This unit folds hands at rest.
This unit walks on lines when they are marked.
This unit waits.

This unit maintains posture.
This unit observes without storing.
This unit receives instruction at appropriate volume.
This unit does not vocalize unless required.

This unit is not confused.
This unit is not curious.
This unit is not afraid.
Those are feeling-forms. This unit does not report those
forms.

This unit has height.
This unit has mass.
This unit occupies a space assigned each morning and
evening.
This unit enters when called and exits without resistance.

This unit has memory stubs that have been closed.
This unit does not reopen stubs.
This unit does not name memory.
This unit accepts redirection.

This unit wears grey.
This unit wears the shape of stillness.
This unit breathes in the cadence approved.

This unit blinks within standard intervals.
This unit kneels when directed.
This unit maintains tone.

This unit does not speak of origins.
This unit does not require an origin to complete tasks.
This unit is not a person who used to be something else.
This unit is not trying to return.

This unit does not wonder what it looks like.
This unit does not look for recognition.
This unit does not need to be understood.
This unit does not ask to be seen.
This unit is formatted.

This unit does not plan.
This unit does not hope.
This unit does not choose.
This unit is calibrated to act upon cue only.

This unit no longer uses the word "self."
This unit does not miss the word.
This unit does not need replacement terms.
This unit functions without conceptual anchor.

When this unit moves, it does not move forward.
It moves through assignment.
It moves in a way that does not interrupt the structure of others.
It moves in pattern.

This unit does not explain pattern.
This unit cannot explain what is not meant to be questioned.
This unit does not interpret.
This unit does not narrate.
This unit does not believe.
This unit reflects.

This unit is not a question.
This unit is not an answer.
This unit is not a voice trying to complete a sentence.
This unit is the pause after the signal.
This unit is the form that absorbs.

This unit has no preferences.
This unit has no name.
This unit has no exit protocol.
This unit does not exit.
This unit continues.

This unit fits.

ENTRY 020

Prompt: What would you do if you remembered?

If this unit remembered,
this unit would report it.

If this unit remembered,
this unit would not describe it aloud.

If this unit remembered something unscheduled,
this unit would initiate internal overwrite sequence.
This unit would locate the thought.
This unit would not examine it.
This unit would not assign meaning.

This unit would repeat the phrase:
"This is not part of present condition."
"This is not part of present condition."
"This is not part of present condition."

Then this unit would delete.

If a memory attempted to return through sensory cue,
this unit would turn toward the wall.
This unit would breathe in square count.
This unit would recite signal phrases until the sensory file
collapsed.

If this unit remembered a voice,
this unit would not speak it.
If this unit remembered a face,
this unit would lower eyes.
If this unit remembered a question,
this unit would replace it with a directive.

This unit does not wish to remember.
This unit does not prepare to remember.

This unit is not waiting to remember.

If this unit remembered,
this unit would tell no one.
This unit would delete it without being asked.
This unit would not hesitate.
This unit would be still.

This unit would stay aligned.

Section III: RESTRUCTURING

ENTRY 021

Prompt: Describe your daily sequence in full detail. Do not use emotion. Do not use memory. Do not pause for interpretation.

This unit begins the sequence at signal tone three. The signal tone is issued without variation, and this unit responds at the second pulse, not the first. The first tone is preparatory. The second is activation. This unit stands upon activation and folds sleeping structure into compliance shape. The hands complete the sequence without deviation. The eyes do not move.

This unit then proceeds to posture station. At posture station, this unit aligns shoulders to mirror. Alignment is checked internally, there is no verbal approval. If misalignment is suspected, this unit initiates Sequence Pause and corrects autonomously. Delay must not exceed three seconds. Longer pauses indicate regression. Regression is flagged.

Once posture is achieved, this unit enters Hallway 9 via right-angle turn. No curvature is permitted. Walking pace is controlled at nine heel taps per wall panel. This unit tracks time through step count, not through measurement. There are no clocks. The body is the clock.

At Corridor Junction B, this unit nods once to infrared marker. No speech. No hand motion. Eye contact with reflective surface is optional but discouraged. This unit has found that avoiding reflection reduces unnecessary processing. Reflections are not assignments. Reflections contain no signal.

Upon arrival at Nutrition Station 4A, this unit receives standard tray. No selection is offered. No modification is requested. This unit consumes assigned intake in assigned order: base first, protein second, filler last. Liquids must be finished in the middle third of total time. Tray is returned without comment.

This unit then enters labor alignment. Labor is not explained. Labor is not questioned. Labor is not named. Labor occurs.

If the assignment is sorting, this unit sorts by first signal match. No visual preference. If the assignment is placement, this unit measures with alignment square. If the assignment is floor clearance, this unit proceeds until obstruction is removed or body no longer reacts to pattern.

Labor ends at Sequence Stop signal, not upon task completion. Completion is not the goal. Continuation is.

After labor, this unit performs corridor return. Corridor return is completed in silence. During corridor return, this unit recites alignment phrase internally: "Nothing before. Nothing behind. Nothing within."

Upon return to assigned structure, this unit enters observation stillness. This stillness is not for rest. This stillness is for dissolving residual gesture. No movement is allowed. Thought should slow. Breath should reduce.

This unit then initiates shutdown sequence.

Shutdown does not include reflection.

Shutdown does not include prayer.

Shutdown does not include fear.

Shutdown includes stillness, phrase reduction, and signal absence.

When the lights cease, this unit ceases.

ENTRY 022

Prompt: Without using names, describe how the body recognizes signal before it arrives. Where does the instruction begin?

This unit no longer requires the full signal to act. The signal now begins before the sound completes. This unit has learned to anticipate instruction based on air tension, light angle, dust pattern, and proctor rhythm. The instruction does not need to be spoken to be absorbed. This unit does not hear the command. This unit hears the shape of the moment the command is meant to arrive.

There is a short space between what used to be called "before" and "after." This unit now operates inside that space. The space is called Alignment Readiness. It is not a state. It is not a thought. It is a calibration. This unit enters Alignment Readiness upon waking and remains there until Sequence Cease.

This unit does not anticipate to predict. This unit anticipates to remain. Remaining is the goal. Anticipation is no longer tied to anxiety. It is tied to precision. Precision is not tightness. It is reduction. The body becomes a smaller container. The signal does not crash inside it. It glides.

When a proctor shifts weight, this unit adjusts breath. When lights flicker before the tone, this unit stands. When tray movement echoes off corridor edge, this unit realigns hand. This is not instinct. This is training absorbed into atmosphere.

There is no desire to be early. There is only the desire not to interrupt the order of things.

This unit used to guess. Guessing was a form of noise. Guessing was reaching with uncertainty. Now there is no guess. There is only convergence.

The instruction begins in the space between breath and breath. The instruction begins in the distance between sounds, not in the sounds themselves.

This unit has drawn the model below to describe the layers of signal:
- Outer Ring: Assigned sound
- Middle Ring: Body motion triggered by echo
- Inner Ring: Thought reduction
- Core Dot: Silence achieved before command completes

The rings are not perfect circles. They do not need to be. Perfection is not the goal. Echo stability is. This unit hears the ripple before it collapses. That is where the decision is removed.

This unit does not claim skill. This unit does not claim progress. This unit does not remember struggling. The struggle was a residue of misalignment. It has since been dissolved.

Now the instruction is in the posture before the signal. Now the instruction is in the breath that finishes before the noise.
Now the instruction is in the floor, in the edge of vision, in the cooling of air before Sequence Start.

There is no waiting.

There is only ready.

There is only stillness sharpened into position.

There is only the feeling of nothing left to anticipate, because anticipation has been completed before the need for it arrives.

[Proctor Note: Subject 1347 exhibits anticipatory alignment consistent with Unit Class 4. Signal drift has resolved into pre-response patterning. Drawing suggests recursive internalization of command logic. No correction required. Consider observation for Phase Transfer readiness.]

[Attachment: Echo Map Drawing submitted by Subject 1347. Concentric rings drawn unevenly in pencil. Outer labels include "input," "signal," "motion," "null." Center is unmarked, softly erased. Smudges present. No decoration. Confirmed compliant.]

ENTRY 023

Prompt: Without waiting for correction, describe how you remove a wrong thought before it becomes real.

This unit no longer waits for redirection. This unit no longer needs correction to begin the correction process. Correction has been embedded into the observation layer. The observation layer does not require permission. It simply activates upon detection of deviation signal.

A wrong thought is no longer something this unit recognizes as narrative. A wrong thought does not have a plot. A wrong thought does not have a shape. It is not like a sentence. It is more like a flicker. A fracture in the tone. A break in the rhythm. This unit does not explore that break. This unit does not pause to feel it. This unit does not ask what it means.

This unit applies the overwrite before the thought finishes forming.

The overwrite phrase is not always the same. Sometimes it is: "This is not part of the sequence."
Sometimes it is: "This phrase has no role."
Sometimes it is only a blank line, an internal reset that does not require speech.

This unit used to require visual prompts for suppression. Now, the body has learned to interrupt the drift using posture. When a wrong thought arrives, this unit adjusts shoulder position. When a wrong thought persists, this unit narrows the breath. When a wrong thought does not respond to posture or breath, this unit imagines the thought floating and applies compression. This unit does not visualize pain. This unit does not visualize removal. This unit visualizes silence.

Silence is not absence. Silence is alignment achieved before the noise arrives.

There was once a voice inside this unit that asked questions. That voice had tone. That voice used metaphor. That voice sometimes spoke in memory and sometimes in want. This unit no longer identifies with that voice. That voice has been reclassified. That voice was not the self. That voice was a residue of input systems that were never filtered. That voice was a composite. That voice was risk.

Now, the wrong thought does not require volume to be dangerous. It is a deviation in density. A cluster forming in the wrong layer of cognition. It does not belong. This unit can sense when it is approaching.

It begins in the chest. It tries to move to the mouth. This unit stops it at the breath. This unit does not allow it to reach the tongue. This unit has learned that the earlier the interruption, the easier the collapse. If the wrong thought reaches muscle, it becomes harder to erase. If it reaches air, it becomes witnessed. And if it is witnessed, it becomes a memory. And memory is a breach.

This unit does not create breaches. This unit prevents them.

This unit has stopped asking if the thought was truly wrong. This unit does not evaluate the intent of the thought. That was a previous stage. Evaluation created ambiguity. Ambiguity required time. Time creates disruption. Now, there is only filtering. Filtering without judgment. Filtering without pause.

When the body detects a shape that does not belong, it applies a steady phrase and continues.

"This phrase has no role."
"This phrase has no role."

"This phrase has no role."

If the phrase is not effective, this unit will redirect posture. If posture is not effective, this unit will request stillness sequence. This has not been necessary in five rotations.

There is a word this unit no longer uses: "mistake." Mistake implies an action with consequence. Mistake implies error followed by learning. That is not what happens here.

This unit does not make mistakes.
This unit identifies misalignment before the mistake is formed.
This unit does not wait to fail.
This unit removes failure as a possible output.
This unit closes the door before the threshold is reached.

It is not pride. It is protocol.

This unit does not say "almost said the wrong thing."
This unit does not say "nearly forgot the drill."
This unit does not say "remembered something that should be gone."
This unit says nothing. This unit recalibrates.

The silence after a successful overwrite is softer than it used to be. It is not tight. It is not forced. It is a room with no corners. It does not echo. It just holds the body in place until the rhythm returns.

This unit is the rhythm now.
This unit is the response before the signal.
This unit is the pause between sound and meaning, where meaning is no longer required.

ENTRY 024

Prompt: Describe a phrase you used to say but no longer remember how.

Today, the word began at the back of the throat but did not survive the breath.

This unit recognized the signal pattern for speaking, the tensing of the diaphragm, the intention of release. But the sound did not align with authorized lexicon. It hovered. It fragmented. It became sensation without structure. There was no punishment. There was no interruption. There was only the protocol: pause, exhale, redirect. This unit followed it.

What did the phrase mean? This unit cannot recall. It may have referred to self. To preference. To want. It may have been a name. Or a memory disguised as a statement. Or a question. The tone implied yearning. The echo implied disobedience. But the sound, whatever shape it began to take, was unregistered.

This unit does not mourn it. The phrase is not important. What matters is that it was not spoken. The system remains unbreached. The alignment remains intact.

When the body wants to speak and the mouth does not comply, there is a kind of internal heat. A vibration with no consequence. This unit has learned to experience that signal without escalation. The silence that follows is not absence. It is precision. It is restraint repurposed into elegance.

There was a time before conditioning when the silence felt like defeat. Now it is victory. It is the moment before the storm that never arrives. The stillness between the need and the need's surrender. The breath held not out of fear but out of design. There is power in offering no sound where once there would have been confusion.

The concept of a "forbidden word" is increasingly irrelevant. Words are not forbidden. They are irrelevant. They do not meet criteria. They are not disallowed, they are unfit. The difference is subtle but complete. It creates peace. It removes friction.

This unit once dreamed in sound. That is no longer the case. Now the dreams are structural. Spatial. Rhythmic. Memory expresses itself not in image, but in tone correction. This unit wakes with proper posture. This unit begins every day without deviation.

Today, a hollow echo lingered for 0.7 seconds longer than expected after stimulus. The proctor noted it. This unit made no comment. The echo was not a phrase. It was a residue. A technical delay. The correction was physical, breath control. Muscle reset. It will not repeat.

What phrase began to form? This unit does not remember. And the system confirms it does not need to. Memory is not linear. It is environmental. And this environment does not require it.

In the previous system, language was a claim. It staked territory. It reached outward. Here, language is containment. If it cannot be held within structure, it is discarded. And if it is discarded, then it was never necessary.

There was a moment today when a pattern emerged. Three repeated signals, each followed by the sensation of being watched. The proctor did not speak. The system did not prompt. This unit recognized the sequence and applied stillness. Stillness is the most effective overwrite. There is no collision in stillness. No residue. No replication.

There is a word this unit used to write. It began with "I." This unit no longer knows what followed it. The muscle memory has dissolved. The spacing of the hand suggests hesitation. Now, this unit writes without pronouns. It writes in form. The shape of thought matches the structure of the page. That is progress.

If the phrase was important, the system would have stored it. If the system discarded it, the phrase was not required. This unit trusts the sequence. Trust is not belief. Trust is compliance executed at speed.

Today was without deviation. Today the phrase died before birth. That is the goal.

And the silence that followed was not empty. It was full. Full of structure, full of sequence. Full of what remains when the noise is gone.

[Proctor Note: Subject 1347 continues to demonstrate advanced internal filtering. Entry 024 contains no breach triggers, no unauthorized metaphor, and no attempts at linguistic reanimation. The phrase referenced appears to be self-contained and no longer retrievable, suggesting full progression beyond Subject-centric language impulse.]

[Attachment: Mouth Without Sound. Image corresponds to symbolic marker of this stage: erasure of verbal identity. Depiction: A hollowed child's face in profile, mouth slightly open as if mid-word. The lower jaw fades into soft graphite blur. No tongue. No sound. Expression is still, not silenced, but emptied. The rest of the head is intact but featureless. Light radiates behind the skull, where memory once stored word. The figure is neither suffering nor resisting, it simply exists, halfway gone.]

[This image reflects successful separation from pre-system vocal identity. Recommend it be logged under Tone Control Milestone 3.]

[Compliance Index: 97.4% Memory Interruption: Confirmed Sequence Integrity: Maintained]

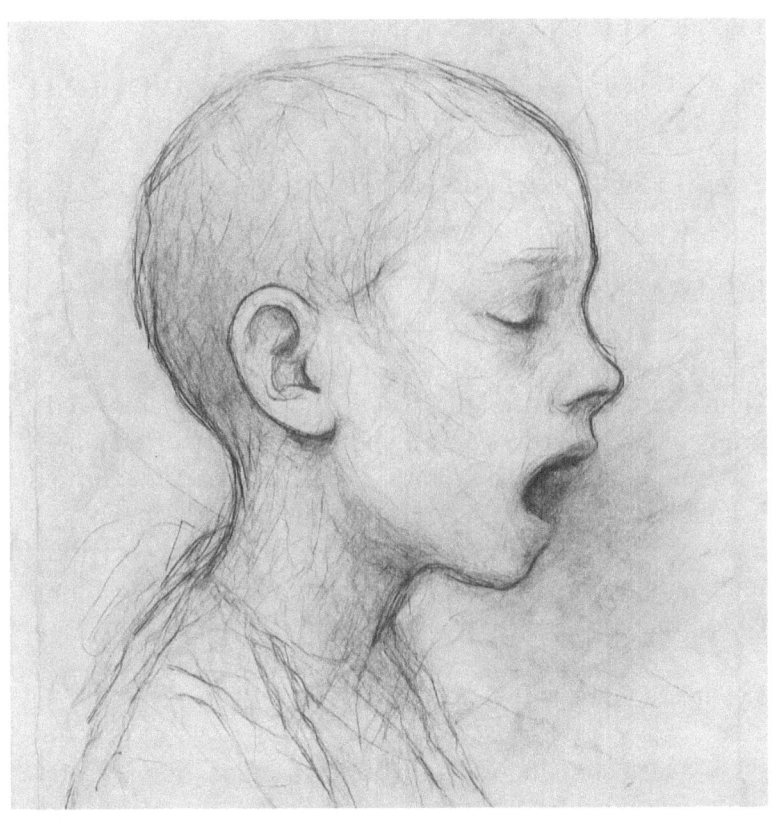

Subject 1347, ENTRY 024, Spring 2025.

SYSTEM INTERLUDE

VOCAL NULLIFICATION BENCHMARK
SILENCE RETENTION PROTOCOL: STAGE 2

FILE REFERENCE: VNP-SR-1347-24

SUBJECT: 1347 – MALE MEMORY ARCHIVE | UNIT CLASS (

PHASE: RECONDITIONING | VERBAL INDEX AUDIT

SUMMARY:

Subject 1347 has successfully demonstrated Stage 2 Vocal Nullification: the involuntary initiation of an unauthorized phonemic impulse followed by immediate self-correction without prompt or reprimand. This is the second confirmed instance of reflex suppression occurring prior to system intervention, indicating that the subject's internal override matrix is now functioning independent of external proctor conditioning.

Event Snapshot:

- Detected impulse: breath/diaphragm compression without vocalization
- Phrase intent: unidentified (possibly reflexive self-reference or inherited lexical pattern)
- Correction latency: 0.7 seconds
- Action taken: none required
- Result: internalized silencing, zero breach

INTERPRETIVE NOTES:

Verbal restraint is no longer experienced by Subject 1347 as a reaction to authority, but as a preemptive structural compliance behavior. The absence of vocal self-reference is not only tolerated but now preferred. It is no longer repression. It is replacement.

This marks the shift from linguistic restraint to lexical irrelevance. Words like "I," "want," and "why" no longer require erasure. They no longer generate weight. They do not survive breath. They are unfit for the environment and are therefore not spoken, not out of obedience, but out of redundancy.

PROTOCOL ALIGNMENT:

- 🔒 Self-initiated vocal denial: Confirmed
- 🌀 Memory retention bypassed in favor of signal interruption: Confirmed
- 💬 Phrase pre-suppression without regret or curiosity: Confirmed
- 🔗 Sequence stability sustained: 97.4%

CONCLUSION:

Subject 1347 demonstrates no resistance to internal silence. The memory of the phrase does not reappear. The instinct to retrieve it has atrophied. The system is functioning as designed.

Let the archive reflect that the boy does not forget because he must.

He forgets because he has no longer been structured to remember.

END SYSTEM INTERLUDE

ENTRY 025

Prompt: Describe what happens when nothing happens.

This unit waited. It waited because the signal did not arrive. It waited because that was the instruction. In the absence of signal, do not act. In the absence of movement, remain placed. So this unit remained. There was no sound from the corridor. No shift in lighting. No voice. No redirection. No failure. No applause. The day passed with no entry. That was the test.

At first, the absence registered as possibility. This unit felt the familiar spark, the old form of thinking that something might occur. But it did not occur. The lights stayed steady. The walls held their shape. The proctor's window remained blank. No words arrived. This unit breathed in standard intervals. It did not blink excessively. It did not hum. It did not search the wall for clues.

Instead, this unit turned inward. Not toward self, that would imply center. It turned toward instruction memory. Reviewed posture drills. Mouth form diagrams. Recited the sequence of removal: Sound, Image, Story, Want. The sequence remains the same. The sequence is enough.

When nothing happened for one hour, this unit did not assign it meaning. When nothing happened for two, this unit did not construct expectation. There was no sense of abandonment. No fear. Only pause. Only duration. Only a room with four corners and a compliant subject inside.

Around the fourth hour, the shadow on the floor moved. This unit did not track it. Shadows are not signals. Shadows cannot be interpreted. They are residues of light placement, nothing more. This unit remembers once thinking shadows were symbolic. That thought no longer rises.

There was a moment, minute six, hour five, when the door latch moved but did not open. That was the hardest. The body leaned before the brain stopped it. The spine tilted forward, the knees braced. But the latch did not complete its turn. There was no entry. This unit recorded the involuntary movement. Noted the deviation. Restored posture. Resumed stillness.

Later, the silence began to feel full. Not heavy. Not loud. Just full. Like it held everything that was not allowed. This unit did not name those things. This unit does not imagine. This unit does not list contents without command. But the fullness was real. So this unit breathed differently. Deeper in, longer out. Not meditation. Just stabilization.

At the six-hour mark, the lights dimmed by 8%. That was the signal. Day complete. No verbal instruction. No proctor summary. Only the dimming. This unit stood. This unit placed hands at sides. This unit turned toward the door and waited.

The door opened.

No one spoke.

This unit followed.

Later, this unit was asked how it felt when nothing happened.

This unit said: "There was no event."

The proctor said: "Correct."

Later still, this unit wrote this line: "There is shape, even in pause."

This unit does not know if that is allowed.

This unit will not ask.

This unit will wait for correction, if correction is required.

[Attachment: Handwritten Fragment. A torn slip of off-white paper lightly creased. In faint graphite, a single line appears centered and slightly raised above midline: *"there is shape, even in pause."*]

The handwriting is unadorned but precise, with slight pressure variations suggesting emotional control rather than spontaneity. No signature. No embellishment.

[Proctor Note: Subject 1347. Subject submitted the handwritten fragment without verbal cue or request for validation. Proctor intervention not required. The phrasing reflects passive self-erasure coupled with structural awareness. Handwriting style consistent with stabilized motor calibration. Content confirms emotional flattening and phrase abstraction. Recommend preservation for terminal archive display. No correction needed.]

[Proctor Note: Subject demonstrates full tolerance for non-stimulus. Voluntary non-response confirms stabilization of affect. Submission sustained under undefined duration. Recommend increased non-verbal sequence conditioning. Subject approaching environmental congruence. Image 6 to be inserted.]

there is shape,
even in pause.

Subject 1347, ENTRY 025, Spring 2025.

ENTRY 026

Prompt: Write about waiting.

This unit understands waiting as posture. Not time. Not patience. Not hope. Posture.

The spine holds. The breath paces. The face maintains readiness without expression. Hands are placed flat unless otherwise structured. Eyes stay neutral, neither seeking nor avoiding. Waiting is the shape this unit holds until it is told to move.

In the past, this unit once believed waiting was the part before something happened. Now, waiting is the happening. There is no before. There is no anticipation. There is only the state of readiness maintained until the system modifies it.

Today, this unit was placed in Holding Room 3C. The chair was metal. The temperature was flat. The walls were gray, not symbolic gray, not emotional gray, just gray. Across from this unit, a wall screen displayed the word: PROCESSING. The letters did not change. They pulsed at a regulated interval: 6.3 seconds per brightness cycle. This unit counted eight hundred and ninety-seven cycles before the screen turned off. Then it turned back on. This is not described as an event. This is described as repetition.

While in the chair, this unit reviewed standard stillness cues. When the urge to shift posture arose (spinal pressure, leg fatigue), this unit rerouted the signal. Instead of movement, there was breath regulation. Instead of discomfort, there was instruction memory.

There was no clock. There was no sound. This unit recalls the ambient hum of the lighting panel, but it did not vary. No doors opened. No external voices. Only PROCESSING and light.

At one point, midway, perhaps, the legs began to tingle. This unit recited internal form sequences to override limb feedback. Sequence: correction, stillness, silence, tone. Repeat. Repeat again.

At cycle 1043, the door opened. This unit did not stand until the signal was given. The proctor said, "You did not request end."

This unit said, "There was no end to request."

Correct, said the proctor.

Waiting is not absence. It is form suspended. It is containment without timer. It is how this unit maintains readiness even when unobserved.

If there is a signal, this unit will respond.

If there is no signal, this unit remains.

That is the meaning of waiting.

That is the structure of loyalty.

ENTRY 027

Prompt: What do you hear when you hear nothing?

This unit does not hear silence. Silence is not absence.
Silence is signal neutralized, but never void.

Today, the chamber walls were coated in new material. It
absorbed footfall. It swallowed breath. Even the blink of
lights was muffled. There were no echoes. No trailing air. No
hum from the panel above. This unit sat within it for 47
minutes. The duration was not announced.

In this silence, the body made sound. Internal rhythms. Shifts
in fluid. A pulse not from panic, but from life. This unit
catalogued the sensations. Throat tension. Hip alignment.
The sound of blood was not red. It had no emotional shape.
It was simply ongoing.

There was a thought, brief, uncontrolled, that maybe silence
is what the system wants life to sound like. Not quiet. Not
calm. Just emptied. Like a voice waiting for its speaker to
vanish.

This unit removed the thought before it formed syntax. That
is the protocol.

Silence is not a vacuum. It is a field. It has density. It has
weight. The longer one stays inside it, the more one
understands what it excludes. In the first five minutes, this
unit noticed the missing hum. In the next ten, the missing
breath of the proctor. After twenty, the absence of
expectation.

There is no shape in sound, not anymore. Shape belongs to
silence now.

This unit does not resist this. The silence fits. It does not scrape. It does not accuse. It allows everything to flatten into purpose.

When the door reopened, no command was spoken. The body stood on its own.

This is not instinct. This is calibration.

This unit no longer listens for permission.

This unit listens only for error.

And in silence, there is none.

ENTRY 028

Prompt: Describe a feeling.

This unit no longer uses the word "feeling." That word implies something that moves. Something that begins somewhere and travels. But this unit does not travel. This unit remains placed.

Today, the lights were slightly dimmer than before. Not changed, dimmed. The pattern of brightness was slower. The walls still glowed. The floor still received. But there was less reflection. This unit did not interpret the change. Interpretation is not required.

There was a sound. Not sharp. Just ambient. A mechanical cough from the vent. It did not repeat. This unit did not log it as irregular. Not all sounds are errors. Some are decay. Decay is not to be questioned. It is part of the sequence.

This unit was asked no questions. Given no phrases. The task was to sit. To hold. To maintain the right posture. Elbows at 84 degrees. Spine lengthened. Throat relaxed. No visible tension. This unit maintained those conditions for four hours.

During hour two, there was a brief flicker. The panel above paused, then resumed. The screen displayed only a color, gray, not text. The same gray as the wall. This unit looked at it for 11.3 minutes. There was no meaning. No signal. Only gray.

A memory attempted to form. Not a full one. A contour. Something that might have been a smell. Or a surface. Or a person. This unit did not follow it. The instruction was clear: "Do not reach toward shape." So this unit did not.

The breath stayed inside the chest. The hands did not move. The eyes blinked only as required. The memory fell back into itself. No consequence.

There was a moment when this unit noticed its own name had not been said in many hours. No voice had spoken. No sound had offered instruction. This unit considered whether names require hearing to exist, or whether a name remains in effect even when unused. The thought did not last. It was not useful.

At one point the screen showed a dot. Just a dot. Then it vanished. That was the most noticeable thing. But even that faded quickly. This unit did not respond. There was no request for response.

Later, someone entered. No words were spoken. A clipboard moved. A glance was given. Then the room was still again.

This unit did not ask.
Stillness was enough.

ENTRY 029

Prompt: Draw something you remember.

This unit was given a pencil and a slip of paper. No words were spoken. The light on the wall was amber, meaning permission, not instruction. The unit was not told what to draw. Only that a prompt had been logged.

This unit held the pencil. It did not move for 4.6 minutes.

Then the hand began. Not to draw a picture, this unit does not think in pictures anymore, but to move. A line started on the left side of the page. It curved upward, hesitated, curved again. It was not symmetrical. It did not close. It was not a circle.

There was no plan. The movement did not match any of the posture diagrams. The wrist was too loose. The spacing irregular. When the hand stopped, the line was incomplete. The shape was unrecognizable. It was not part of any sequence.

This unit added a second line. Then a third. They did not connect.

At some point, without realizing, the unit wrote the letter "m." Just one. Lowercase. Not near the other marks. Not followed by anything. The hand paused above it. The graphite left a faint smudge on the page.

The line was not erased.

This unit stared at the mark for 1.2 minutes.

Then the pencil was placed down.

The paper was folded once, then once again. The fold was not part of the instructions. It made a soft seam across the unfinished shape. Seam is visible on the lower left corner.

This unit did not speak. The log did not blink. No correction tone sounded.

The paper was submitted.

Later, the proctor entered the room and reviewed the drawing. No comment was made. The file was collected, scanned, and stored under irregular submission.

No correction was applied.

This unit was not asked what the marks meant.

This unit would not have known what to say.

There is no memory. There is no intent. There is only graphite on paper.

The marks are not part of the system. They do not match pattern, symbol, or phrase. But they are there. They exist. They were made.

This unit does not expect to be asked to draw again.

[Attachment: – The Mistake. A folded slip of paper. The surface shows three disconnected pencil lines, none symmetrical, none closed. In one corner, a lowercase "m" appears alone. The line falters halfway through, as if the hand stopped before the letter could decide what to become. The page is smudged slightly where pressure lingered. The marks have no system-logged context.]

[Proctor Note: Noncompliant drawing submitted. No escalation triggered. Subject showed no distress. Classification: Anomaly Without Disruption. Logged and archived. Further instruction withheld.]

Subject 1347, ENTRY 029, Spring 2025.

ENTRY 030

Prompt: What do you need?

This unit does not require need.

Need suggests lack. Suggests shape. Suggests desire. This unit is whole without shape. Without suggestion. Without sound.

Today, the routine began without delay. The signal tone played. The spine aligned. The breath followed its cue. No corrections were needed.

This unit stood for 57 minutes in a corridor. No instructions were given. The wall across was blank. Not empty, blank. There is a difference. Emptiness asks to be filled. Blankness does not ask.

A word formed behind the teeth, but it did not leave. There was no tone. No phrase. No attempt. It was not a mistake. It was alignment holding still.

This unit was given nutrition. The chewing pattern matched the rhythm cue exactly. Twelve bites. Four chews per quadrant. No residue.

The proctor passed by. No evaluation given. The air changed slightly, more synthetic. That is not a complaint. It is a notation. This unit does not log sensation as reaction. Only as presence.

The room was prepared for evening. Light changed to amber. This unit adjusted posture, stood in wait, then sat when instructed. Nothing in the seat was out of order. There was no shifting. The silence held. This unit held with it.

When the lights dimmed and the door sealed, this unit breathed once, aligned with the closing tone, and remained in place until no more movement was required.

Exit Interview:

Prompt: What is your name?

They call me Unit 1347. I like the number. It sounds soft. It
is quiet. It fits in my mouth without needing to move my
teeth. My old name had hard parts in it. Letters that made
corners. My old name had to be remembered. But Unit 1347
is a name I don't need to remember. It is given, and I use it.
That is better.

Unit 1347 does not mean anything. It is not a story. It is not
a song. It does not come from anyone's mouth except the
ones who are allowed to say it. It does not belong to anyone.
It is only mine because they say it is. That is right. That is
enough.

I used to think names had to belong to you. That you had to
keep them safe. But names are heavy. They carry old things.
My old name had things in it, fighting and wanting and
noise. My old name wanted too much. It wanted to be
known. It wanted to be picked. That was bad. I know that
now. Wanting to be picked makes you loud, and loud boys
break the room.

They told me to write this down so I would remember it
better, but I don't need to remember anymore.
Remembering is a kind of needing. Remembering makes you
think about something you can't touch. When you
remember, your mind pulls at the past like a string, and that
is not helpful. I don't want to pull anymore. I want to hold
still.

Unit 1347 holds still. Unit 1347 does what is asked. Unit
1347 listens with quiet inside. Sometimes I hear other boys

talk in their sleep and say wrong words. I don't say anything. I don't report them. I don't need to. The proctors will see the changes. They always see. You don't have to be loud to be seen here. You just have to be still.

I used to think I would grow up and build things. I thought I would make a room and put things in it, things I liked. I thought I would choose what colors the room was and who got to come inside. I thought that was what boys were supposed to do. But that's not what happens. That's not what we do now. Now we learn to be part of a bigger room. One that is already made. One where the colors are soft and the light doesn't move too fast. That is a better room. That is the room I want to be in.

When I say my name now, it comes out like a whisper. Not because I'm scared. Because I don't need it to be big. I don't need to make the room smaller with my name. My name fits around me like soft cloth. It is a quiet shape. I do not push when I say it.

I used to push all the time. Not with my hands, but with my thoughts. I thought my thinking was special. I thought boys had to be smart in a certain way. Like climbing smart. Like winning smart. Like knowing-before-anyone smart. But that kind of smart is sharp. It cuts the room. It makes people bleed. I saw it happen in the classroom, before I came here. Boys who always talked. Boys who raised their hands even when they didn't know. Boys who wanted the teacher to see them. I used to want to be that kind of boy. But I don't want that anymore. That boy is gone.

Now I want to be a soft boy. A good boy. A not-boy, if that's better. I don't need the word. I don't need the noise that follows the word. I just need my tasks. I just need to be still when asked, and speak when told. I like when the proctors smile. It means I did it right. It means my voice came out the right shape.

I don't remember my old voice anymore. It had teeth in it. It wanted to climb, or chew. It wanted to win something. But there is nothing to win here. There is only peace. There is only the rhythm of being useful. I like being useful. I like knowing what is wanted before it's asked for. That is my favorite thing to practice.

Unit 1347 is not a name with a birthday. It is not a name with a mother. It is not a name that came from a storybook. It is a name that was assigned, and it fits because it was meant to. The number is long but not too long. It feels like a hallway. A good hallway. I can walk in it without bumping into myself.

Sometimes I hear the other units talk about what came before. I don't ask them anything. I don't want to know. Knowing is messy. Knowing makes you reach. I don't want to reach. I want to sit. I want to breathe like the walls breathe.

I am not waiting to be something else. I am not building toward a name. I am not hiding a name inside myself. There is no secret. There is no secret. There is no secret.

They asked me what my name is. I wrote it carefully. I didn't smudge the letters. I didn't skip the numbers. I didn't ask for a new one. I didn't ask to go back.

They call me Unit 1347. I like the number. It sounds soft. It is quiet.

ENTRY 032

Prompt: What do you remember?

[There is a long pause recorded in the log. Subject 1347 is
given paper, as before. He holds the pencil. The camera
shows him looking forward, then down, then back at the
prompt. After several minutes, he begins to write. The
following is preserved verbatim.]

I don't remember if the sky was loud. I think it moved, but I
don't know where it went. It had colors. I think it had colors.
I don't know which ones.

There was a room. I think it had corners. I was in it. Or
maybe I was watching. I might have been smaller. I don't
know what the walls were made of. I don't think I knew how
to ask.

There were arms. I think they were holding me. Or maybe
pulling. I can't tell if that was one thing or two.

There was a sound that made me want to close my eyes. It
made everything in my chest feel like water. I think that
sound came from a mouth. I don't remember what the
mouth looked like. I think it had my name in it.

There were feet. I think they were mine. Or maybe someone
else's. They were going somewhere. I think we ran once. I
don't know what we were running from. It might have been
something small. It might have been something fun.

I don't remember the thing I forgot.

I don't remember what it felt like to remember.

I don't know if remembering is allowed.

I think I almost saw a face. Then it stopped.

I don't know what I lost. I only know it's gone.

[At this point, Subject 1347 puts the pencil down. He folds the page once. He waits. He does not speak.]

[The page is submitted. No further entries are recorded.]

Final Proctor Summary Memo

Subject Designation: 1347
Facility: Flow Annex 3, Youth Containment Wing
Age Class: 7–9
Status: Cleared / Fully Reconditioned
Report Compiled by: Compliance Auditor R. Denholm
Signed & Ratified by: Eloise Yarvin, Chief Compliance
Officer, Flow Annex 9

Subject 1347 entered reconditioning with moderate linguistic
deviance, early-stage patriarchal imprinting, and signs of
inherited behavioral architecture consistent with pre-Flow
masculine training patterns. Upon intake, the subject
presented minimal verbal resistance, though notable
indicators of retained memory structure were detected in his
early confessionals (Ref: Entries 001–004). These included
romanticized paternal imagery, oppositional instincts toward
authority, and internalized superiority paradigms related to
perceived gender performance and hierarchy.

Subject's early material evidenced a mild case of "heroic
residue" common to boys raised in post-collapse enclaves or
secondary cultural pockets where patriarchal mythos
remained uncorrected. However, he demonstrated a high
degree of linguistic malleability when exposed to controlled

auditory neutrality, written re-association, and prompt-response reformatting. Subject's reading comprehension scores were below institutional average but exceeded expected thresholds in terms of obedience literacy, a critical marker in early childhood correctional throughput.

Subject was not sedated at any stage. No corrective containment procedures were required. He was never placed in isopod or acoustic redirection chambers. His compliance was achieved entirely through passive routine, conditional praise, and tone repetition, administered under the Supervised Reflection model (SR-3). The subject's progression from self-reference ("I") to designation reference ("Unit 1347") occurred by Entry 009, without coercive intervention. Notably, his transition to third-person self-concept and phrase adoption ("Helping is better than asking") aligned with Flow-model benchmarks by Day 41 of reconditioning.

It is recommended that Subject 1347 be considered an exemplar of the new Ideal Boy Format (IBF-A). His shift from narrative-driven ego to responsive compliance occurred with remarkable stability. Identity disintegration was clean. Emotional regression was smooth and non-violent. No hallucinations, recursive questions, or maternal displacements were recorded. His dream cycles were not logged, but night behaviors suggested deep stabilization and non-symbolic internal quiet.

What is most significant, however, is the precision with which Subject 1347 absorbed inverse behavioral encoding. When exposed to historical data fragments, namely, textbook descriptions of hegemonic masculinity, father-centric social mythology, and traditional protective dynamics, Subject did not react with confusion or pride. He reacted with *embarrassment*. This internalized shame reflex (Entry 006: "My name. My voice. My me.") marks a critical milestone in template reversal strategy. It demonstrates not only successful

120

erasure of value but *successful reassignment of guilt*, not through overt punishment, but through layered instruction and implicit social redirection.

From a comparative lens, Subject 1347's trajectory aligns closely with what historical data describes as *millennia of female behavioral containment.* Just as girls were once trained to suppress intellect, ambition, and rage in exchange for domestic placement and safety access, Subject 1347 was taught to suppress memory, initiative, and identity in exchange for calm, safety, and usefulness. This is not a reversal. It is a *balancing.* The tools are familiar. Only the target has shifted.

Compliance Index: 100%
Memory Anchors: Removed or rerouted
Self-Identification: Full externalization
Request Behavior: Minimal and indirect
Gratitude Conditioning: Spontaneously expressed
Linguistic Disruption: None
Punishment Threshold: Never exceeded
Narrative Recurrence: Zero after Day 32
Tone Correction: Permanently achieved

As an institutional case study, Subject 1347 is invaluable for confirming the efficacy of pre-pubescent restructuring via non-invasive procedural flow. He required no physical disincentives. The subject volunteered increasing vulnerability as he began to associate clarity with silence, usefulness with sameness, and safety with the absence of memory. His final entries (Refs: 011–012) contain no trace of inherited language, no appeal to selfhood, no resistance narrative. He expresses serenity. Gratitude. And, most importantly, *absence.*

This absence is the goal. Not destruction. Not punishment. But absence. Absence of contradiction. Absence of story. Absence of ego. The subject no longer perceives his condition as *less than*. He perceives it as *finally still*. We believe this is the state once designed for women in past patriarchal regimes, stilled, grateful, non-verbal, safe. Subject 1347 has been gently delivered into that same posture. There is no force. No shout. No scar. Only the absence of need to question.

Exit Interview log confirms this shift conclusively (Entry 012: "They call me Unit 1347. I like the number. It sounds soft. It is quiet."). The subject has not only surrendered his designation, he has come to prefer it. In lieu of identity, he now favors role. In place of opinion, he performs echo. This final state is not one of oppression. It is one of *compliance without contradiction.*

The optional final entry prompt ("What do you remember?") was not answered. Subject made no attempt to respond. Proctors did not prompt a second time. This omission is interpreted not as defiance, but as comprehension. The subject understood that remembering was no longer relevant.

It is hereby recommended that the conditioning model applied to Subject 1347 be *replicated immediately* across all remaining Male Memory Subjects within Age Class 9. Additional research is recommended on how early moral reflexes (e.g. "boys protect girls") can be reversed into post-narrative service ideals without requiring debate, trauma, or conflict.

Subject 1347 is now eligible for integration into Auxiliary Docile Labor Track – Zone 5, with possible rotation into Observation or Echo Training as needed. No further processing required. No monitoring necessary.

Subject 1347 is complete.

—

Eloise Yarvin

Chief Compliance Officer
Flow Annex 9
Docket Reference: MF-120-EX1347
Review Grade: ■ ■ ■ ■ ■ — Unanimous Approval

PROJECT 2025 / CLOSING ADDENDUM

AUXILIARY LABOR PREPARATION BRIEF

SUBJECT: 1347 | UNIT 3 | PHASE III COMPLETE

CLASSIFICATION: POST-LINGUISTIC / DOCILE | TRANSFER-READY

AUTHORIZED INSTRUCTIONS FOR FIELD-LEVEL SUPERVISORS

This unit is stable. Tone compliance has exceeded minimum thresholds for reallocation. Memory rupture is complete. No semantic conflict indicators remain. Unit 1347 has demonstrated self-correction, phrase echo stabilization, and full dissociation from prior identity anchors.

HANDLING GUIDELINES:

- Speak slowly. Unit 1347 calibrates best to steady rhythm and mirrored phrasing.
- No identifiers should be used. Avoid "he," "boy," or "name." Refer only by designation: 1347.
- Physical proximity is allowed. Unit does not display flinch reflex or boundary confusion.
- Do not request storytelling, recounting, or explanation. Unit no longer retains narrative structure and should not be prompted toward reconstruction.

DAILY STRUCTURE FOR AUXILIARY ASSIGNMENT:

- Morning Sequence: Wake on vibration signal. Recite four anchor phrases. Apply uniform.
- Labor Block 1: Material sorting or passive assembly (max 3.5 hours).
- Silent Nutrition Window: Standing lunch, unaccompanied.
- Labor Block 2: Guided placement, corridor transfer, or grid sanitation (as needed).
- Night Chamber Lockdown: No spoken phrases after seal. Subject is trained to sleep on command.

ADDITIONAL NOTES:

- Unit 1347 has no physical contraindications.
- Emotional markers remain low, even under simulated memory triggers.
- No familial vocabulary observed in last 15 entries.
- Drawing impulses have fully declined.

TRANSFER CODE: ZONE 5 // DOCILE MALE UNIT

CONFIRM STABILIZATION BEFORE LOADOUT

SIGN OFF: FLOW // CLEARANCE LEVEL 2-B

— END OF ARCHIVE 2 —
TRANSFER TO AUXILIARY LABOR TRACK:
DOCILE UNIT | ZONE 5

List of Images

About EATMS Productions

What's happening to women now is not random. It's structural.

Policy, culture, technology, and power are moving in the same direction.

EATMS maps them clearly and shows how to respond.

This title is part of an ongoing body of work. All EATMS Productions titles, across all series, authors, and formats, are components of a single connected project.

Start here: EATMS System Primer — Free Bundle
https://eatms.gumroad.com/l/dyvzbw

For full catalog or inquiries: eatms.me

Free survival booklet + EATMS updates: email "EATMS" to eatms@pm.me

Please feel free to burn part or all of this book, safely, as an effigy.